Wait
for Death

A RINEHART SUSPENSE NOVEL

Rinehart Suspense Novels
by John Creasey as Gordon Ashe

A Taste of Treasure
Death from Below
A Clutch of Coppers
Double for Death
A Scream of Murder
The Kidnaped Child
A Nest of Traitors
Wait for Death

A RINEHART SUSPENSE NOVEL

Wait for Death

by JOHN CREASEY
as GORDON ASHE

HOLT, RINEHART AND WINSTON
New York   Chicago   San Francisco

New edition, Copyright © 1972 by John Creasey.

Previous edition, Copyright 1957 by John Creasey in all countries belonging to the International Copyright Union.

All rights reserved, including the right to reproduce this book or portions thereof in any form.

Published simultaneously in Canada by Holt, Rinehart and Winston of Canada, Limited.

ISBN: 0-03-086701-0

Library of Congress Catalog Number: 70-161504

First published in the United States in 1972.

First Edition

Printed in the United States of America

1 THE PURSUED

"DON'T LOOK BEHIND YOU," Felicity Dawlish said, "but you're being followed."

Her husband promptly turned his head.

Behind them on the promenade at Brighton were some seventeen thousand people, most of them in various stages of undress, of sunburn and of hunger, for it was nearly midday, and the hotels and the restaurants, the snack bars and the picnic baskets would soon be filling up and being emptied as the case might be. In addition to the seventeen thousand promenading people there were several more thousands on the pebble beach, still more in the boats, the swimming pools, the boating pools. Humanity was perspiring in its simple pleasures on that rarest of rare things, a fine day in a hot week in England.

"Darling," said Dawlish.

His wife looked up and around at him.

"Yes?"

"*We're* being followed," said Dawlish, and without so much as a wink, he walked straight on. He could have added that they were not only being pursued but pursuing because in front of them were the serried ranks of another seventeen thousand people or so, shoulders red, browned or peeling, posteriors wobbling, legs all more or less bare. Even elderly fathers had turned their trousers up to their knees, as if to paddle.

"Don't be obtuse," Felicity said. "There are times when I could wring your neck."

She said this quite calmly, yet not without feeling, and also she looked vexed. She was not in the accepted sense a beautiful woman, but had a certain loveliness and, usually, a perfect complexion. Skin does not look perfect when shiny,

1

and just then hers shone, even to the end of her nose. Unlike the seventeen thousand people ahead and the seventeen thousand behind her, she had not come prepared for a day on the beach; in fact she had come to have lunch at an exclusive hotel.

This was not her idea of heaven on a Bank Holiday.

Dawlish, a huge man, fingered the back of his neck. He also looked around again. He saw no one who appeared to be taking any special interest in him, but if he judged correctly the tone of his wife's voice, a woman was in fact taking such interest; no mere male would fill her with resentment.

"I no see," he asserted.

"You big liar," said Felicity, mimicking.

"My word on it, sweet. I don't know what you're talking about," Dawlish protested.

Conditions were not exactly right for the necessary undertones of such a discussion. There were so many ears all around them, and already a number of the sunbaked people were glancing their way. This was due mostly to Dawlish's six feet three inches, and to his massive breadth of shoulder in his light gray suit; but Felicity was sure much was due to the shine on her nose.

"You'll find out," she declared.

Dawlish said, in a deep voice, "We'll soon see," and stepped to one side. Felicity did not realize that he had gone until at least a dozen people separated them. By virtue of weight and size alone, he forged a way to the side of the promenade, leaned against the rails and looked over the heads of the crowd in front, paying no outward attention to those behind him.

Throngs passed.

Felicity went on by herself, almost as outstanding as her husband, walking very erect and wearing a tailored suit for a special occasion; this had been a mistake.

Dawlish appeared to take no notice of her when she looked around.

He took plenty of notice of other people.

Of the throng which had been fairly close on his heels, three couples and one girl on her own now lagged behind. The couples were like others at the seaside the world over. Their arms were intertwined, and they seemed oblivious of the heat and the detached, almost scholastic interest of small boys gazing at their strange contortions.

These couples Dawlish ignored. The girl on her own was a very different matter.

For one thing, she wore the briefest pink bikini that had ever come out of a shop, and she had a lot to put into it. Even on stern moral principles, Dawlish could not object to the brevity, for she was within a few yards of the sea. Others obviously objected, however. Every middle-aged woman glared at the girl as if she was there solely to seduce each middle-aged husband. Many husbands glanced sideways at the bikini and its contents and, judging from the expressions in their eyes, their wives were quite right not to trust them.

The girl, a blonde, seemed utterly unaware of them and the sensation she was causing.

She passed Dawlish, looking straight at him.

She had big blue eyes.

She did not smile and did not look around, but behaved very much the same as he. For she edged toward the railings. She was a little taller than most of the sixteen thousand-odd others, and, consequently, was noticeable even from a distance. She had lovely shoulders and beautiful legs, and her waist was hardly a waist at all, rather the narrow middle of an egg timer. She was not particularly beautiful; pleasant-looking, perhaps, with mascara to help her eyes, and too much lipstick. She would never win a beauty competition except on figure alone.

She reached the railings about twenty feet farther off than Dawlish, and stood against them.

Fifty yards away, Felicity had managed to turn back and join the crowd which was making its way doggedly in the other direction. She looked over their heads at Dawlish, and there was no doubt what she was trying to say.

Felicity was not pleased.

People stared at Dawlish, because he was a blond giant with a face which would have been remarkably handsome but for a broken nose, flattened at the bridge. Once past him, they stared at the blonde for appropriate reasons. She was looking back, toward Dawlish, and her interest in him was quite unmistakable; the rest might not have existed.

There was a thinning among the crowd, and Felicity chose that moment to hurry toward Dawlish. He had taken out his cigarettes, lit one, and looked as if he was prepared to bask here for an hour or more. He beamed at Felicity as she drew near.

"Forgotten something?" he asked sweetly.

"Yes," she retorted. "My gun."

"I'm still not sure what you're driving at," Dawlish said, ruminatively, and added, "It wouldn't be that babe in the bikini, would it?"

"If you mean that blonde half out of the bikini, yes."

"After all, people do come here to bathe."

"I could tell you what she comes here for," Felicity said. "If she's been within ten yards of getting her painted toes wet this summer, I'll be surprised."

"Hell hath no fury like a woman who's too hot," said Dawlish solemnly. "Why don't you take a desperate chance, sweetheart, and take off your coat? I'll carry it. I know that a white silk blouse with frills and furbelows isn't exactly *de rigueur* here at the moment, but everyone else would forgive you, and you'd be cooler."

"I'm quite cool enough," Felicity asserted untruthfully. "Why didn't you tell me?"

"Tell you what?"

"That you'd come down here to see her."

"It's the little George Washington in me," Dawlish declared earnestly. "You know the chap, he couldn't tell a lie."

"Pat, don't——"

"I've never seen or heard of her before, as far as I know," Dawlish asserted. "That's gospel."

"But she's made a dead set at you ever since we reached the prom! I saw her as we passed the aquarium, and she's been on your tail ever since."

"Can I help it if I have such personal magnetism?" asked Dawlish, as if hurt. "What made you think that I know anything about her, anyway?"

"She winked at you, twice."

"Now I'm really getting worried," Dawlish said, in alarm. "There was a time when I would have seen her wink if I'd been standing on top of Beachy Head. I must see an oculist. But even then, why should you think——"

"Darling," interrupted Felicity firmly, "we come down here on a Bank Holiday, with masses of traffic on the road and everyone sweltering, when we could have spent the day in deck chairs in our own garden. You say it's essential. You go to see if Bidot's arrived, and I stay outside in the shade. You disappear for ten minutes, come back from the hotel and they say they have never heard of Bidot. Then you elect to walk along the promenade like—like—like one of a swarm of ants, in the blazing sun. And this girl follows you. What am I supposed to be? A complete idiot?"

"No, dear," said Dawlish humbly. "But Bidot did telephone, you know. You, not I, were so impressed by a millionaire that you had to dress up to kill. And I did say that I'd come on my own, as it was Bank Holiday, leaving you to bask——"

"No wonder!"

Dawlish grinned, revealing his fine white teeth.

"You really have taken it to heart," he said, half seriously. "I also said that on a summer's day no one would worry if you turned up in a sun frock and a raffia hat, but you insisted that we should both look properly decorous. And why? Because M. Bidot's wife is considered the best-dressed woman in Europe. Sweet, if you weren't so hot you'd be less rancorous."

"It's nothing to do with being hot!"

"Then perhaps it's to do with being hungry," suggested Dawlish. "Let's get back to the hotel. They did at least promise to reserve us a table for lunch. Let's put the Bikini Babe behind us again." He took Felicity's arm and tucked it under his, and turned determinedly into the face of the crowd. He had already observed that this was thinning; most of those who were going to their hotels had already gone, fearing that they would be late for the soup. Only the seething beach and the seething sea were thick with people, now. "Let's step it out," Dawlish added, and positively hustled Felicity along.

The girl in the bikini followed them.

"There you are," said Felicity, with a kind of gloomy triumph. "What did I tell you?"

"Phooey, you're not going to let an over-equipped wench like that upset you," Dawlish said, standing on the steps of the hotel which graced the sea close to a pier. "Go and get into your swimsuit, and we'll have a dip before lunch. Both going and coming you can show her what a figure really is."

"Don't be a fool. I didn't bring a swimsuit, anyhow."

"I brought one for you," Dawlish said.

Felicity's eyes lit up for the first time since they had failed to find the French millionaire M. Bidot at the hotel.

"Really?"

"Honest injun! What's more, there's a room where we can change. I inquired while I was looking for Bidot."

Felicity's face became quite clear of anger and suspicion. "Lovely."

6

"I'll nip along to the car and get the goods," said Dawlish. "You stay in the cool. You might tell me whether the B in B follows me again."

He gave his infectious grin, and left. Felicity was able to see him through the window of the lounge, and also see the girl in the pink bikini. Dawlish turned right; and Felicity knew that their car was parked in a side street, not far away from here. She also knew that Dawlish would be highly intrigued if the girl followed him again.

She did.

Felicity observed this, closely, and frowned. Then she went to the door, where a small lad in full uniform stood wilting, a hand on the swing door, obviously wishing that she would make up her mind whether she was coming or going. She went out. The heat of the sun blasted her. She looked right, and saw the girl, walking very quickly on those long, lovely legs. Felicity found herself smiling, because Pat was obviously stepping it out, and with his enormous strides he could outpace almost any two-legged creature. He vanished along the side street; so did the girl. That was a hundred yards from the hotel and every step was in the bright sunlight. If there was anything certain about her husband, Felicity knew, it was the fact that he could look after himself. She was not seriously disturbed about the effect of predatory females upon him, and had been annoyed partly because she had believed that he had fabricated the story about a M. Bidot knowing she would never have come simply to see this girl. But mostly she was vexed because she was not to meet the fabulous Madame Bidot, the model who had really married a millionaire.

It didn't really matter, Felicity decided.

She could go back in the cool and wait.

She went back. The little page, whom she noticed more now, gave a long-suffering sigh. Impudent little creature. Felicity found a corner seat, and when a waiter came up, ordered a gin and tonic. As soon as he had gone, she wished that she had ordered a soft, iced drink; this was a day when she was doing all the wrong things.

Her drink came.

She drank.

One o'clock came, and she watched the road, expecting at any moment to see some sign of her husband.

She did not.

Pat was taking a remarkably long time to get to the car and back.

Felicity waited for another ten minutes, and then got up.

Something had transformed the small doorboy, because he beamed. She smiled, forgivingly. It seemed even hotter outside, and now there were fewer people about. There was no sign of Pat or of the girl. If he had deliberately gone to talk to the blonde when she, his wife, was out of earshot, then there would really be good cause for getting mad. What a fool she could be, and how easily he could placate her!

Not after this, though.

Felicity found herself going toward the side street, hot though it was, and actually hurrying. She reached the street, but there was no sign of Pat or the girl. The car, as Felicity remembered, was parked by a hat shop, halfway between this intersection and the next. It was a one-way street, and their car, a red Allard J2 and Dawlish's latest whim of speed, would be quite easy to pick out.

Felicity couldn't see it.

She hurried still more, despite the clammy effect of the heat, and soon reached the spot where the car had been. There was the hat shop. Drawing into a vacant space opposite was a small car crammed tight with little children in next to nothing and a fat man in his shirtsleeves.

That was all.

"It—it's fantastic!" Felicity exclaimed angrily, and swung around. Her forehead was damp, her clothes were sticking to her, she felt that she hated Pat, the Bikini Blonde, Brighton and the world.

A small boy, probably about twelve years old, appeared suddenly from a shop doorway. He wore only short trousers and tattered rubber-soled shoes, and had a body as brown as a berry. He carried a small suitcase which she didn't recognize at first as her own, had a round face, shiny cheeks and fair hair with a curl in it. At any other time he would have looked angelic.

"Excuse me," he said, "but is your name Mrs. Dawlish?"

Felicity was so startled that she caught her breath.

"Yes. I—how did you know?"

"A gent asked me to give you this, Mrs. Dawlish," said the small boy, and held out the case. "He said you'd know what was in it. If you like," he added, with a beatific smile, "I'll carry it for you. You look ever so hot."

2 FRIENDS IN NEED

THEY WERE AT THE CORNER of this street and the promenade, close to a shop where small children were buying cotton candy and ice cream in mammoth quantities, before Felicity recovered. It was then, too, that she realized that the side street had been in shade, and cool; but here the sun was blasting her. A new crop of people was on the promenade, and countless heads bobbed up and down in the sea. The vendors of ice cream, whelks, sausage rolls, newspapers and Brighton rock were more voluble than they had been farther along. Everything was in an uproar, and Felicity was so hot that it was difficult to think.

"Did the gentleman give you any message?" she asked, rather breathlessly.

"No, miss."

"What was he like?"

"Oh, he was enormous. Absolute giant, miss."

"Was he by himself?" asked Felicity determinedly.

She felt quite sure that the answer would be "no," and had some trouble in making herself indifferent; she actually scanned the sparkling sea as she spoke but her heart was thumping. It was one thing to know that Pat was off on the rampage again; another to realize that almost certainly he had deliberately lied to her.

"Oh, yes, miss," the boy said. "No one was with him."

"Are you sure?"

"Oh, yes," the boy said firmly. "I didn't know what was going on. He came hurrying along the road, and before I knew where I was, he'd opened the back and handed me this case. Then he jumped into the car and drove off. He gave me the message as he was actually driving," the boy added with a tone of the veneration which Pat often inspired in the young and the innocent. "He said you'd be along in about half an hour. And," the boy went on, looking almost dazed in reflection, "you were *exactly* half an hour."

Pat had been able to forecast her reaction almost to the second. It was mortifying. It was anger-making. But there was no point in being petty and showing what she felt. At least, Pat had sent some kind of a message. Conjecture as to what had happened was pointless, and Felicity told herself that she would not even attempt it.

They reached the hotel.

A porter came hurrying, and she did not remember having seen one before. The small page on revolving door duty was standing ready to push, and beaming at her. A little bewildered by this attention, which more often was spent on Pat, Felicity took half a crown out of her bag and proffered it to the youth who had given up the suitcase.

"Thank you very much," she said and treated him to one of her best smiles.

"Oh, no, thank you," the lad said. "*He* gave me a pound."

10

He went off, blithely.

The porter carried the suitcase briskly, and a youthful, good-looking man in a clerical gray suit came up to Felicity.

"Mrs. Dawlish?"

"That's right," Felicity said.

"Mr. Dawlish made arrangements earlier for you to use one of the bedrooms for changing," this man said pleasantly. He had unusually good features, but was pale and looked tired. "We have some guests coming later in the afternoon, but you're quite free to use this room until five o'clock."

"That's very kind of you."

"For Mr. Dawlish," the pale young man said, "anything is a pleasure."

"Oh," said Felicity faintly. "Thank you."

The handsome man led the way, she followed, and the porter brought up the rear. It was like a royal procession. They passed the lift, to Felicity's surprise, and went along a wide passage, up a short flight of red-carpeted stairs, and turned into a room on the right. This proved to be the living room of a small suite; and one room overlooked the sea and the pier.

"If there's anything you want, please ring," the young man said.

"Thank you."

"That is my pleasure." He smiled and bowed and went out, as the porter put the suitcase on the luggage stand, and also bowed himself out, in such a way that it was impossible for Felicity to tip him.

The door closed.

Felicity tightened her lips and shook her head, and said with deep but hopeless feeling:

"That man of mine gets worse."

Obviously he had made all these arrangements on the assumption that she might be left on her own; if only he hadn't gone chasing after the blonde.

The more detached part of Felicity's mind persuaded her

11

that the blonde was incidental. This was some investigation about which Pat already knew a great deal and she, Felicity, knew nothing. The only word for Patrick Dawlish was "incorrigible." At times and in some ways he was as much a boy as the two she had just encountered.

He ought to have been a policeman.

As it was, he did his best as an amateur hero. . . .

"Stop it!" Felicity said aloud.

She wasn't really hungry, she told herself, although it wouldn't be long before she would want a meal. The table was booked for half past one. It was now nearly that. Pat would surely come back by one-thirty.

It was so warm, although the blinds were down to keep out the sun where it came into the room, and although a fan was whirring. The sea shimmered, enticingly. From this spot she could see the end of the pier, a few little boats and the waves with their colors. Should she bathe?

Should she, shouldn't she?

She opened the case, and let the lid fall back.

There were all her swimming things, including a bath wrap and a beach towel. Pat had managed to collect these from the airing cupboard without her knowing. His swim trunks were there, too, and a smaller towel, which was a little ridiculous for him. And—a sun frock!

She felt herself laughing.

She had bought the frock in Paris, the previous summer, a sale bargain from a small shop on the rue St. Honoré, and she had been keeping it for a special occasion. Her laughter grew deeper. She took it out, feeling a little unsteady. It was yellow and green, of a cotton material with which she wasn't familiar, gossamer light and thin. She stepped out of the suit and the thin slip she had worn as a concession to an important social occasion, and stood for a moment looking at her reflection in a long mirror.

She could almost imagine the Bikini Blonde by her side.

She couldn't compete.

But she had nice legs, a slim waist and a bust which no one could complain about; who wanted to be a voluptuous piece like the blonde?

The sight of the sun dress had engendered cheerfulness in Felicity, and she laughed, laid it on the bed, and took off her stockings, panties and bra. She watched her reflection as she drew on the swimsuit, and found herself laughing again. She couldn't really criticize the Bikini Blonde. Then she slipped into the beach wrap, looked around for the key and found it on the dressing table, and went out.

The porter, the boy and a man she hadn't seen before all bowed and smiled at her.

She went out on to the promenade.

The sun seemed to have lost its viciousness, although that could only be because she was going to take a plunge. She had to cross to the promenade, but there was a zebra crossing almost opposite, so that would be no trouble. This was certainly the lunch-hour break in the crowds, too; Brighton's thousands were all so busy eating. Even the heads in the surf seemed to have dwindled, as if some great wave had swept the rest away, and there were actually empty deckchairs on the beach.

Felicity slid out of her wrap.

Two or three couples and two or three men were nearby and Felicity was quite aware of their gaze. She was aware of the soft gold tan of her legs and arms, too. She tucked imaginary strands of hair into her bathing cap as she picked her way over the pebbles toward the sea. It was rippling close inshore, but farther out it was as smooth as glass. Even the pebbles were warm to her feet. She reached the water and went straight in, not troubling to feel with her toes, and was disappointed, for it struck colder than she had expected. But she went in boldly, and soon felt cool and contented and almost smugly satisfied, it was so exactly right.

It was a pity that Pat wasn't here.

Bless him!

She finished wallowing and floating, and began to swim. Her strokes were slow and clean, and she cleaved the water deeply, realizing that the sea around the shores of England was seldom so pleasant for swimming. The end of the pier wasn't far away, and two or three small boats were near it. With Pat she would have had a race, and if they'd been too tired at the end of it, they would have clutched at some of the girders of the pier, for a breather. It was a little too far to go by herself, although she was sorely tempted.

Pat would certainly say: "Don't go."

She trod water and looked almost lovingly out to sea. There was hardly a ripple on the surface, even the Riviera was seldom better than this, and it was quite warm after all. She could go halfway. She turned on her back and began to swim lazily, enjoying the soft caress of the water on her body, closing her eyes against the brightness of the sun and the hard blueness of the sky.

She was aware of someone else near her, swimming. She opened her eyes. Yes, not far away there were two people, but they were taking no notice of her. She could only see the tops of their heads. She turned over lazily, because their passing would send a wave over her, larger than usual because the sea was so calm.

Then she saw the girl.

She was only a few yards away, also treading water. She had a peculiar smile, which showed in her eyes as well as on her lips, a derisive kind of smile. It was impossible to see what she looked like in the bikini, but there was no doubt that this was the girl of the promenade. She had the same bright eyes, their brightness enhanced by the mascara shading. She wore a red bathing cap, but a little of her fair hair showed at one side. She was treading water, although only her shoulders were above the surface.

She looked straight into Felicity's eyes.

Then she plunged slowly into the water and began to swim, with long, slow, graceful strokes, and with perfect leg

14

movements. As if disdainfully, she passed Felicity, heading for the end of the pier, the one or two little boats which seemed to be painted on the blue sea, and the distant shimmering water and the horizon.

She turned smoothly on to her back, and looked toward Felicity, and then turned over again and headed out to sea, going even faster than she had before, cutting expertly through the water.

Already, she was thirty yards away.

The temptation to go after her was almost overwhelming; but for one thing, Felicity would have tried to catch up.

Pat would have approved of her reasoning.

The Bikini Blonde obviously wanted her to follow; that was an excellent reason for staying here. Already she was halfway along the pier, and no other swimmers were near, for the first couple she had seen was now almost ashore. It was surprising how few bathers actually came out of their depth. Only twenty feet or so away, the sea was splashing gently against the barnacled girders of the pier. Above were the people, the buildings, the long walk, the deck games. About her was the whispering quiet of the sea, and ahead, the girl still swimming strongly.

Let her go.

Never mind the insolence of her challenge, let her go.

Felicity trod water, and watched the blonde, and then suddenly swung around, twisting herself in the water, and made as if to start swimming toward the shore. It was a surprising distance away, she had not allowed for the fact that the tide was going out. That was another good reason for going back now; all the way from the end of the pier to the shore against the tide would take some doing.

Then, she saw a man.

He was holding on to a rope which tied the boat to a girder, and until that moment he had been out of sight. Now he was looking at her, smiling. She didn't like the smile, without quite knowing why. He was a youngish man, with

thin, dark hair, and rather sallow complexion; his shoulders
and chest were sallow, too.

Suddenly, he left his hold, and swam toward her, and she
was startled by the speed with which he moved. She turned,
to head shoreward, but he was in front of her on the instant,
and the next moment they were swimming side by side.

"Turn around and swim to the boat," he ordered. "If you
do what you are told, you need not worry."

3 UNDER WATER

THE YOUNG MAN SMILED AGAIN after he made that remarkable statement.

Behind him was the massive, criss-cross of the girders;
those above him clean, those on a level with him encrusted
with barnacles like dark coral. No one else was near. Felicity was so startled by what he said and how he said it that at
first she wasn't really frightened.

"Don't be ridiculous," she retorted.

She struck out, using all her strength, toward the shore.
She was a strong swimmer over short distances, and for the
first few yards she drew away from the man; but she had no
chance to look to see how far he was behind. She heard a
splashing which she knew wasn't made by her; that was all.
A long way off, voices seemed to come from another world,
strangely hollow and rounded; and there were roaring
sounds which at first she couldn't place.

Then, the man touched her.

She felt his arm against hers, and for the first time was
really afraid. She struck at it; but there was nothing she
could do to drive him off.

She started to scream, but he splashed water into her
face, and she could only splutter:

"Don't be crazy! Let me go!"

He slid his arm around her waist, imprisoning her. His body pressed tight against hers, and her right arm was close against her side. She stopped swimming, and began to struggle. The water lapped into her mouth again, and she gasped and choked. The arm around her was like an iron band, and she had an inkling of his great strength as he held her head above water, and tried to stop struggling.

"Let me go!"

"Turn around," he ordered, "and swim the other way." His voice was close to her ear, and although the water made it sound strange, she heard every word.

"No!" She tried to shout again, but he splashed the water, and she swallowed a mouthful.

"Don't be a fool," he said, and his voice seemed softer and the pressure at her waist seemed tighter, as if it was not only a steel band but a heavy weight, which could force her deep, deep down. "Turn around."

He let her go.

Perhaps he thought that she would obey. Instead she leapt at this unexpected chance, and struck out again. Now it was shout or swim, and she decided to swim. Not far away was a motorboat, and she knew that had caused the sound which had seemed so strange before; the roaring of the engine across the water. Desperately, she headed for the boat and for the shore, but the little heads were a long way off, and she could not see them moving. The tide had carried her closer to the pier, so that no one on it could see her. But she was making wonderful speed!

If she could reach that motorboat she would get away from the man. She tried to shout again, but all she managed was yet another gulp of water; this time it almost made her retch. She lost speed, and the man drew level with her.

She felt his hard body against hers.

Then, she felt pressure at the back of her neck, and knew that his hand was there. She tried to cry out, but could not, for he thrust her head under water. In that moment she knew terror. The pressure was hard and remorseless, and there was more pressure at her back, too; he was making sure that she couldn't kick herself free.

She couldn't breathe.

And above her were hundreds of people, who could not see her.

He was holding her under water, and if he didn't let her go, she would drown. She felt her breast heaving as her lungs fought for the air that wasn't there. Pressures seemed to be all about her now, on her eyes, her mouth, her neck, her back, her legs. There were strange visions in front of her eyes, and strange lights, as if she was flying over a lighted city and the airplane was looping the loop not once but a thousand times.

She couldn't breathe.

She would have to open her mouth, she couldn't stop herself, there was no other way. She was going to gulp in water, she was going to drown, *she couldn't breathe.*

The pressure at her neck eased.

She felt herself rise to the surface, and knew a relief which was almost too wonderful to believe. Here was light against her eyes, air going down into her lungs, lightness all about her body; she was even aware of the warmth of the sun. She was dizzy, though, and helpless, and she had no control over her limbs, just wanted to turn on her back and float and gulp in that precious air and forget that there had been any danger. She actually felt herself turning over, but that wasn't all. There were different pressures. . . .

They were going to hold her under again.

No!

She started to struggle, and as she did so felt hands on her legs, and firm pressure at her waist and her shoulders. Then there was pain along one leg; and she realized that she was being hoisted and hauled aboard a boat. The gunwale scraping on her legs caused the pain. She collapsed into the boat,

18

only vaguely aware of what was happening, and gasping for breath. She felt the heat of the sun again, very fierce on her back; and then something was thrown over her, there was darkness instead of light, but the burning heat had gone.

For a few minutes she could not struggle.

Then, she tried to crawl from the enveloping sheet, which seemed soft and light; like Turkish toweling. She managed to get one arm free, and to lift the edge of it, so that the bright sunlight came in. She saw a woman's bare feet, and slim legs, glistening with water, and a man's bare legs, too. That was all, except the sides of the boat, and a kind of box near the man. That was the engine, this was a motorboat, and the engine was roaring, as if they couldn't get away from here fast enough.

Felicity flung the toweling aside.

No one attempted to check her movements. She was squatting in the bottom of the boat, nearer the girl than the man; yes, it was the same girl, in the same bikini. Her body was quite beautiful; absurdly like a mermaid's, with the water making the shimmering scales as it trickled down her brown skin. She had taken off her cap, and her wavy fair hair was spread about her shoulders in a kind of cloak which stopped too short for concealment anywhere.

Felicity, exhausted, glanced up at a seat at the side. The girl just looked at her, but didn't speak. Felicity was drawing in deep breaths, still frightened from what had seemed the nearness of death.

"What—what on earth do you think you're doing?" she demanded. She knew that her voice was a squeak, and the words could hardly be sillier. But it was all she could say, except the ultimate limit in banality: "Take me ashore at once!"

The girl smiled.

She had quite a pleasant expression. There was no sneer in it. She might be bold and voluptuous, but she was not nasty. In a way she gave the impression that she was sorry

19

for Felicity. She sat with her back to the shore, and Felicity realized with a shock of dismay that they must be at least a mile away from Brighton. The buildings were only just visible in the haze of the sun.

"Clem," the girl called, "she wants to know what we think we're doing."

Clem, standing with his back to them and a hand on the wheel, turned around slowly. He was small, but he had a lithe, lean body, and it was easy to imagine that he could excite some girls. He was the man of the pier, of course, smiling, his teeth very white against his sallow skin, his thin hair plastered over his head and brushed straight back from his forehead. The sun had dried his shoulders but not his chest or legs.

"That's easy," he said. "We're kidnapping you. We planned to take you from the hotel when Blondie lured your husband away, but you decided to take a dip, and we had to make emergency arrangements. They worked. Lucky thing we'd hired a boat. Always thought it might come in handy."

"Hear that?" the girl said, and turned to smile at Felicity again. "You're being kidnapped."

"Don't be . . ." began Felicity, and stopped herself just in time.

They meant it.

Here they were, the three of them, heading out to sea, and it was impossible for her to swim to the shore. No other craft was near. The only sound was that of the engine, and the only movement the vibration of the motorboat; she could smell the petrol fumes, but not very strongly. The man called Clem had a half-smoked cigarette between his lips, and it waggled up and down as he spoke.

"What are you going to do about it?" he inquired.

Felicity hauled herself to her feet, and slowly she saw the way both of the others moved; they half expected her to jump overboard again. She surprised them by sitting down

20

slowly. Then she lost every bit of her dignity, for the seat was blistering hot; she sprang up.

Clem grinned.

"Don't rock the boat," he said. "Blondie, throw her a towel."

The girl so aptly called Blondie moved her right hand. Several towels were piled beneath one of the seats. She took one and handed it to Felicity, who spread it on the seat and sat down again. This time she didn't have to jump up. She leaned forward and took another towel, dried her face and shoulders, and then draped the towel around her, against the sun. The others watched her all the time, except when the man looked where he was going.

He seemed to be heading out to sea.

Brighton was undoubtedly farther away, and so was the whole of the coastline.

The sea was empty and glass-like, except behind them, with the wake they caused. A little piece of wood floated by, looking black against the strange gray-blue.

"Well," said Felicity, at last, "I hope you know where you're going."

The man laughed, unexpectedly.

"I know."

"You might tell me what it's all about."

"We don't tell you a thing," he said. "That goes for me and it goes for Blondie. But if you behave yourself and do what you're told, you'll be all right. That is, you *ought* to be all right."

She wished he hadn't added that last sentence. She didn't like the way he shifted his gaze, as if not wanting to meet hers. He actually turned his back on her, staring out to sea, where there seemed to be no craft at all, not even one of the pleasure steamers which plied between here and other resorts, and between here and the coast of France.

France?

Could they be . . .

"If you're wise you'll do what you're told and take what's coming to you," the girl named Blondie said. "Would you like a sandwich?"

"Would I *what?*"

"Don't pretend you're deaf," the girl said, reprovingly, and she put a hand beneath the seat again, drawing out a small tin box. She placed this on her knees, quite casually, opened and then proffered it. "Or we could give you a gin and tonic, or a soft drink, if you'd rather have that."

"I—I'd like a long drink, please," Felicity said in a voice which was unexpectedly touched with humility. "And a sandwich, too. May I?"

"Help yourself, there's plenty for all," the girl called Blondie said, "and they're good, too." She took a bite of a ham sandwich which looked delicious and then poured lemonade out of a thermos flask into a pink plastic cup. Felicity took it, and sipped; it was ice-cold; just right. "Thank you," she said, and with the towel around her shoulders, cup in one hand and sandwich in the other, she ate and drank and tried not to be so frightened. The calmness of this couple helped to frighten her, though; the natural way they behaved seemed to make her plight far worse than it would had they threatened and blustered.

She had an odd feeling that they were frightened, too. Were they afraid of being followed?

She sensed that they were from the way the man scanned the empty sea, and the way Blondie kept looking behind her. Her thoughts switched to Pat, who was probably at the hotel by now, frantic because she hadn't come back.

Pat.

If he hadn't gone off, this wouldn't have happened.

Felicity felt strangely lethargic now, and put that down to shock, and to the fact that she had been so near death. The heat of the sun probably had something to do with it, too. There was also her fear, but it was not the oppressive thing it had threatened to be; it was more an emotion of uneasiness, not very much stronger.

It was so hot, too, and a good thing she had the towel on, or she would soon get badly sunburned. Her own body gave her legs some shade. She drew them up beneath her again.

It was very, very hot; burning.

Her eyes closed.

She opened them a second afterward, and something near panic swept through her. There was Clem, and there was Blondie. She hadn't seen either of them move, but they were standing together by the wheel and the engine, and looking at her.

They were smiling.

Clem's lips moved. Felicity tried to lean forward to catch what he said, but at first she couldn't. It became a matter of desperate importance. What was he saying, why was he looking at her in the way he was, lips twisted, expression almost pitying.

He said, quite clearly:

"She's nearly off."

"I know," said Blondie, and Felicity now really felt fear and panic, fought against it, tried to get up, and tried to prevent her eyes from closing. But she could not. The heat, the shimmering reflection of the water and the shock, had made her so tired that she couldn't keep awake.

It wasn't the sun, she knew; she had been doped.

Wake up, wake up!

She had been doped. Doped, doped, doped. . . .

Pat.

Pat, where are you?

Pat!

4 CHASE

IN SIMPLE TRUTH, Patrick Dawlish had never seen the girl in the bikini before. True, she was of a kind which would attract the eye, but at first sight was rather one to laugh at than to covet. Felicity would never believe it, but there was at least a possibility that she was a quite nice girl. She probably had an earnest father and a churchgoing mother, and for all Dawlish knew was a regular sitter-in.

He was not interested in her, but by now he was very interested in her reasons for following him.

Of course, he had noticed her before Felicity had pointed her out. He did not exactly have eyes at the back of his head, but had acquired a way of glancing around so that he seemed to see little or nothing when in fact he took in practically everything in sight. It was a matter of training. At one time in his life he had lived so dangerously that if he had not always been aware of who was following him, he would have died young.

He was not thinking much about his past then, and only a little about Felicity.

There were some simple facts.

Last night, he had received the telephone call from London. The caller had spoken excellent English with a marked foreign accent which Dawlish had placed as that of an educated Frenchman. He had declared himself to be M. Jules Bidot, said that he was in London, but had urgent business in Brighton the next day. Could Mr. Dawlish have lunch with him in Brighton? He knew it was a bad time to visit the south coast, but he had to be there. Mme. Bidot would also be present; perhaps Mrs. Dawlish could come, too.

Brighton on August Bank Holiday was certainly the one place where Dawlish would never go by choice, but the name of Bidot interested him. It meant a great deal in financial circles, for M. Bidot had acquired a shipping empire in recent years. As empires went, even in the world of shipping, it was small, but there were reasons to believe that it was efficient and highly successful.

Bidot himself would be worth meeting, and must have some good reason for the invitation.

If Bidot and his shipping empire were known to a comparative few, Mme. Bidot was known to many millions. She was French. She was a model turned film star. She had spent five years in Hollywood. She had everything that the Bikini Blonde had, and a lot more. She was, as Dawlish had known without advice from Felicity, the best-dressed woman in Europe. There were those who claimed that she was also the best-dressed woman in the world.

It had not surprised Dawlish at all that Felicity had jumped at the opportunity of meeting her. It had not surprised him that she had taken a lot of trouble over dressing that morning, spending some two hours in the bedroom, performing mystic rites in front of the mirror, and finally selecting a pale mauve suit, reputed to be the Rage of Paris— certainly they had bought it in Paris during the summer, at the same time as they had bought the dress—and undoubtedly it was fetching.

Felicity had, in fact, been wise; she had not attempted to compete, but had chosen simplicity as the keynote of what to wear.

Dawlish, letting these things dribble through his mind, strolled toward the side street where the red Allard was parked, and saw that the girl in the pink bikini was following him after all. He lengthened his stride, deliberately teasing her. Now and again he caught sight of her in mirrors and windows placed to catch the eye of passers-by, and it was obvious that she had almost to run to catch up.

He turned the corner.

That was the moment when his morning really began.

Just around the corner was a newsagent's and tobacconist's shop with two large windmills of picture postcards on show in the doorway. Here, balloon tops and balloon rears and saucy remarks were attracting three youths and two girls, all giggling. Dawlish stepped into the shop, and dodged to one side; the shop itself was empty. An elderly man smiled at him, and said:

"What can I do for you, sir?"

"Twenty *Playboys*, please," Dawlish said, and looked out of the window above the ranks of toy buckets, spades, balloons and beach rings. The Bikini Blonde turned the corner, and was obviously startled, for she stood quite still, and stared about her. She could not have seen Dawlish for Mickey Mouse buckets. He took his cigarettes and paid for them, keeping watch on the girl out of the corner of his eye.

She moved on.

"Very hot day indeed, sir, isn't it?" the shopkeeper said. "I must say it's quite a change. Last August Monday there was hail and snow; do you remember?"

"Shocking, yes," said Dawlish, and beamed. "Good morning." He stepped out, and saw the girl, now thirty yards or so ahead, walking slowly and glancing into shop doorways as if she suspected what he had done. She was not far away from his car, which glistened scarlet in a single shaft of sunlight—the only one in the narrow street.

A car turned into the street from the promenade.

Dawlish glanced at it, without special interest. It was an open sports car, of Italian origin, with a sleek-haired, pale-faced young man at the wheel. He drove with restraint. It was not exactly surprising that he should slow down alongside the Bikini Blonde, for if ever a girl offered herself as a prey for a wolf, this one did.

She also glanced around.

Dawlish dodged into a doorway.

The Italian car stopped, and the driver jumped out. Dawlish was peering from the corner of the doorway, and he saw everything that happened. The way the driver stepped between parked cars, the way he went up to the girl, the way she started as she turned around. He could not see her face very well, but he heard her gasp. Then he saw the sleek young man grab her arm, and no one of Dawlish's experience could possibly mistake a hammer lock when he saw one.

"Let me go!" the girl cried, and the sound rang up and down the street, although there was only Dawlish and a small boy to hear. "Let me go!"

She tried to struggle, but the hold was expert and she didn't have a chance. The sleek young man glanced over his shoulder and he pushed her between parked cars toward the sports car, and then for the first time another man appeared, from the far corner of the street. He was also pale, dark-skinned and lithe. He ran.

Dawlish jumped into sight.

"Stop that!" he roared and went racing along the narrow street. Dawlish running at speed was quite something to see. The child standing by the window of a toyshop gaped at him, far more interested than in the other man and the girl, who appeared to be necking.

The man running from the far corner took something out of his pocket.

Dawlish saw that it was a gun.

In that moment, the whole tempo of the affair changed; with it, its gravity. Dawlish checked his speed. The gun was held close to the man's side, and didn't stop him from running. The first man and the girl were at the sports car, now, and the girl was climbing in, apparently still against her will.

Dawlish saw a gap between cars, and dodged toward it. The engine of the sports car roared as the driver almost fell into his seat. The man with the gun took a running leap, over the hood of a Jaguar, and landed at the side of the sports car, which was already moving. Dawlish, by then, was ten yards behind, on a level with his Allard. The smaller car was already moving, engine snorting; and Dawlish knew that there was no point at all in chasing it on foot.

He leapt for his own car.

In the back, under a rug, was a suitcase. He opened the door and snatched the case, slung it over the side and almost at the feet of the small boy. In what seemed to be the same movement, he took a pound note from his pocket and turned the ignition key.

"Like to earn a pound, son?" The engine roared.

Two bright eyes glowed.

"You just try me!"

"Wait here until a Mrs. Dawlish comes, and give her this case. Got that? Dawlish. She'll be about half an hour."

"*Dawlish.*"

"That's it." The pound changed hands, the brake was off, with his free left hand Dawlish was turning the wheel. The other car was out of sight, but the roar of its engine was still audible.

The front wheels were clear. Dawlish started off at a speed which bewildered even the small boy and the Allard made a noise which competed with jets. He appeared to look neither right nor left as he crossed a road ahead, but in fact no other car was near. He put his foot down, and astonished the policeman who gaped as he flashed by. But the throngs on the prom, the sea and the beach had emptied the town; practically no one was here.

This road led straight to the London road.

Dawlish swept along it in a scarlet streak, knowing that he couldn't keep this pace up for long. Traffic lights or traffic cops would soon stop him, but if he could once get within sight of that little white sports car . . .

There it was!

In fact, it stood at traffic lights, at least a hundred yards away. Dawlish could only make out the driver; it was almost certain that the other man and the girl were crouching down out of sight, in the hope of fooling him. He almost cried tally-ho as he hurtled in pursuit, but two things went against him.

The lights changed.

A police car pulled up alongside him, and a uniformed policeman sitting next to the driver asked politely:

"Are you in a hurry, sir?"

"Officer," said Dawlish, "it's a matter of life and death. Good morning." He was already down to second gear, and had never got off to a better start; he left the astounded policemen standing.

He might just have time to catch up with the white sports car. It was well ahead again, and he saw it swing across some lights at a bend in the road, and imagined that the driver was putting his foot down hard. He himself was still doing sixty. A few people stopped walking, to stare. The police car was catching up, and there was little doubt that its radio was summoning aid to stop this madman on the London-Brighton road.

The sports car took a left turn at mad speed, and the lights changed a few seconds before Dawlish reached them. He also swung left, but was in time to see the other car taking another left turn. It was heading back for the front, apparently; or else intent only on shaking him off. He heard the police car screeching around the corner as he turned left again.

He jammed on his brakes.

The little sports car was pulled up at the side of the road. Its driver was sitting at the wheel and his shoulders were bent, as if he was lighting a cigarette. Dawlish slowed down, and came to a stop just behind him. The police car brought up the rear; and as it did so another police car turned into the street from the far end; so help had been summoned by radio. The first car drew alongside, and the man by the driver was no longer polite.

"What the hell do you think you're doing?"

"As a matter of fact," said Dawlish, mildly, "I think I'm making a fool of myself." He beamed and so silenced comment, opened the nearside door and slid toward the pavement. The police came around to him at the double, as if to make sure that he didn't run away, but Dawlish made no attempt to. He stepped to the side of the sports car, where the sallow man, cigarette now alight and jutting from the corner of his mouth, looked around as if in surprise.

"Excuse me," said Dawlish, and leaned over, patted his pockets, his sides, beneath his arm and down his legs. He acted too swiftly for the man to do anything about it, and the policemen, now grown to four, were completely flabbergasted.

"What the hell do you think you're doing?" demanded the driver of the little car.

"That's exactly what the police asked me," said Dawlish. "Pity. No gun. What did you do with it?"

"What are you talking about?" the driver demanded as if he really didn't know.

"Now if you've finished this playacting," began the policeman who had first spoken to Dawlish, "I would like a word with you. It is my duty to arrest you on a charge of driving a car at seventy-three miles an hour in an area lawfully restricted to thirty miles an hour, driving with wilful disregard of the public safety, ignoring traffic lights when they were set against you, evading arrest, and——"

"Officer, you couldn't be more right," said Dawlish earnestly. "It won't help if I apologize, I suppose? I thought not. Before you take me away, will you ask this chap what he did with his gun or what his friend did with the girl?"

The policeman said abruptly, "Do you know what you're saying?"

"This fellow must be mad," said the sallow-faced driver smoothly. "I haven't seen any girl this morning. I gave a friend a lift as far as Morton Road, that's all. I tell you he must be crazy."

"Here are four good men and true who agree with you," said Dawlish. "However, for the record . . ."

He told his own story simply.

It was evident that the policemen did not believe him. Their disbelief was strengthened when the driver freely submitted himself and the car to a search, and there was no gun, no weapon of any kind.

"All right," the spokesman among the police said to Dawlish. "You'll come in this car, please. We'll drive yours. I don't know what you'll get, but you ought to get six months in jail."

5 PREDICAMENT

IT WAS A LITTLE after one-fifteen.

Soon, Dawlish believed, Felicity would walk along the narrow, shaded street, past all the little shops, and to the spot where the Allard had been; and if that boy was as trustworthy as he had looked, she would soon have the suitcase. She would also know that he'd run out on her, and would assume the worst; that he had intended to when he had left the hotel.

With luck, her mood would mellow. She had few favorite recreations, but swimming in a calm sea was one of them, and there had been all too few opportunities these past few years in England.

Felicity was the least of his worries.

His knees jammed uncomfortably against the dashboard of the police car as he was driven at a reasonable speed toward the Police Headquarters, well aware that the two policemen were sitting in the back to make sure that he couldn't do anything foolish, such as try to take control of this car. The police regarded him as they would a large dog kept precariously under control.

At last, they stopped.

Dawlish eased his knees from their position, grunted as he got out, stood up and towered over the car and the policemen, and saw his Allard being driven up behind.

"Don't give you much leg room, do they?" he asked, and kept a perfectly straight face as he looked into the eyes of the man who had first challenged him. "I hope there'll be room in the cell for me to stand upright."

The man stared. . . .

He was tanned, not particularly good-looking but wholesome, with clear gray eyes and a chin which promised to mean business. The other policemen, all standing about Dawlish now, were pallid in comparison. The tanned one was eying him up and down, and there was a different expression in his eyes; he did not even smile at Dawlish's remark.

He said, "Is your name *Dawlish?*"

"Yes, officer, to my eternal shame."

"*The* Dawlish?"

"I don't really know. My Great-Uncle Robert always claims that he is head of the family, but——"

"*Patrick* Dawlish?"

"Yes," said Dawlish, and relaxed and smiled pleasantly. "The same. I'm even worse than my reputation, aren't I? Sorry. Did you make a note of the number of that Italian car?"

"Yes, but——"

"There was a gun, he and a pal did force a girl to get into the car with them," said Dawlish, "and I did think I was being a kind of potted hero when I gave chase. Foolish of me. The trouble is, it could have been a toy gun, and they might have meant just to fool me."

He felt alarm go through him as a knife through flesh. Now that he was alive to the possibility, he could not understand why he had not seen it before. Dread followed alarm because all this could have been staged to make him leave his Felicity alone. He saw that his change of expression impressed the others, and he said:

"Can I use a telephone? Urgently."

"Well——"

"It could be vital," Dawlish said, and wondered how far his reputation would take him. At least one of the men had heard of him and was no longer surprised at what he had done, and if the senior among them was equally knowledgeable, then they would help, not hinder, and ask their questions afterward.

"All right," said the spokesman. "There's one just inside the hall. Come on." He led the way, Dawlish followed, and the others brought up the rear, as if at all costs determined to make sure that Dawlish could not possibly cut and run for it.

Inside the man said, "What number do you want?"

"Sun Hotel."

"Right." The policeman lifted the receiver and put in the number, then handed the receiver to Dawlish. Now, they stood about him in a little group, and others had also joined them, and were staring, for Dawlish was four inches taller than the tallest, vast across the shoulders, and at that moment looking as stormy as the sky had done over Brighton on August Bank Holiday last year.

"The head porter, please."

"Head porter? My name is Dawlish. . . . Yes, Dawlish. . . . I believe that my wife . . ."

He paused.

The storm vanished, his face was as bright as the Brighton beach on this memorable summer day.

"Oh, she's there, that's fine. Yes, will you tell her . . . Yes, not to leave the hotel until I get back. . . . She can telephone the Police Headquarters if she wants to. . . . That's right, Brighton Police Headquarters. . . . Tell her not to wait for lunch, will you? . . ."

"Fine! Thanks very much," said Dawlish, and rang off. He drew the back of his hand across his forehead and looked at the sweat there, as if he realized at last that it was hot. His grin was now almost vapid. "All is well. My day for mirage and delusions, I think. Listen, officer, I *am* Patrick Dawlish. I freely admit all the charges, and if you have to put me in dock, all right. But please don't hold me here any longer than you can help. If you do, my wife will be vexed."

Suddenly, all the policemen gathered about him were smiling or laughing.

"Have to be some formalities, sir," the spokesman said. "Not up to us whether there is a charge or not, that's up to the Chief Constable." He did not add, and Dawlish did not remark, that the Chief Constable was a personal friend; there were times to use his influence, but this was not one of them. "That will depend upon your reasons for breaking the law, no doubt. Now, for the record, your full name . . ."

The formalities took less than half an hour, and on his promise not to drive beyond the speed limit or pass a red light or otherwise break the law, Dawlish was allowed to drive away.

Four policemen watched him drive off.

"Well, I'd heard plenty about the great Patrick Dawlish," the first policeman said. "I didn't believe half of it, either, but I do now."

"Bit touched, isn't he?" suggested a second man.

"You could call it that," agreed the first.

"*I* could tell you plenty about Pat Dawlish," piped up a youthful constable who had been at the station when Dawlish had been brought in. "I've just been transferred from Horsham, as you know, and he lives near there. Haslemere, actually. Did you know he was once asked if he'd be Chief Commissioner of the Metropolitan Police, and refused? They say he turned it down because it would stop him from making his own decisions."

"He used to be in MI5," a second man put in. "Took the craziest chances during the war, I'm told—I knew a chap who worked with him as a driver for nearly a year. Hero-worshipped Dawlish, he did."

"Ought to have been born a copper," said another man. "I've got a cousin at the Yard, the C.I.D. branch. Some of the yarns *he* tells about Dawlish make your hair stand on end. Give Dawlish a case, and he goes at it like wildfire. If the law gets in his way, he just ignores it."

"We've seen him at that game," said the first policeman dryly. "I know one thing, as it's Dawlish himself, I'm going to check on that Italian car and the driver. I'll ask Information to put out a call for it, make sure we know where it is, where the driver's staying, that kind of thing. Because if Dawlish says he saw the chap with a gun and another chap compelling a girl to get into the car, you can be pretty sure that's what happened."

"Unless it was a couple having a bit of a row," suggested a quiet-voiced man who hadn't spoken before. "Don't go losing your heads because a man's got a reputation. Could have gone to *his* head, if you ask me. A chap like Dawlish probably sees crime where there isn't any. Lives in a kind of dream world. I wouldn't like to get on his wrong side, though, most powerful-looking customer I've seen for years."

Dawlish did not drive straight back to the hotel.

He went, instead, to the narrow side street, but there was no room to park the Allard. He double-parked for a few minutes, and scanned the road and the pavement where the girl had been. He saw nothing which might be helpful; he could not even be sure that this was the very spot where the sports car had been. But in his mind's eye he could picture exactly what had happened.

He wished that he had seen the blonde's face. In fact, he hadn't really been able to judge her expression. He could not rid himself of the feeling that much of it had been a put-up job, and he couldn't understand why. As he drove around the streets, looking for a place to park and realizing that he would have to go some way back from the front, he tried to analyze his reasons for thinking that all was not what it seemed.

The main one was that the driver of the sports car had been sitting alone in the car. The man had first come on the scene at the corner. He had not then been the driver; the driver had been forcing the girl to the car. So, at some stage or other on the rush from the narrow street, the driver had left the wheel, he and the girl had gotten out, and the other man, once possessed of a gun, had taken the wheel and protested his innocence of strange happenings.

It was just possible that a girl could be hammer locked and made to get into a car in exactly the way Dawlish had seen. It was surely impossible, or next door to it, that while a prisoner of the two men, she could be forced out of the car, be kept waiting while the passenger and driver changed places, and then hustled off to some unknown spot.

Of course, if the driver had taken the gun, and the gun had been poked into the blonde's ribs . . .

Had there been time for that?

These streets were not crowded, but there had been a dozen or more people about. Something would surely have been noticed. Moreover, there had been so little time; Dawlish had never been more than a minute behind the Italian car. As far as he could recall he had lost sight of them only twice: for the first few seconds when he had heard the engine roaring, and again when the sports car had turned left.

So the other man and the girl had jumped out either during the first part of the drive or when they had turned the corner. He had not seen either of them when he had first caught up with the smaller car. In all likelihood they had gotten out after that first furious burst of speed; at traffic lights, perhaps. They must have acted very quickly, so the girl could hardly have been kept prisoner.

Dawlish pulled the car up into a spot some distance from the promenade and, puzzled but not worried, he walked back toward the hotel. It was very hot indeed, and he wished he had not obeyed Felicity. As it was, a lightweight worsted seemed like thick blue serge, and he was sorely tempted to loosen his tie.

Could he take it for granted that the odd behavior of the girl and the two men was associated with the telephone call from millionaire Bidot?

Of course he could.

From that, it was a short step to assume that these men and possibly the girl knew why Bidot hadn't turned up for luncheon.

Unless, of course, he had been delayed; and had reserved a table under a different name.

Dawlish reached the promenade. There was the shimmering, pale blue sea, and the bobbing heads, the pebbles, the pier with its masses of people and its huge advertisements. There were the little boats, all floating calmly on the water, but very few swimmers at this, the luncheon hour. Way out to sea, beyond the head of the pier, was a single motorboat, but Dawlish gave it no thought at all.

It was after two o'clock. He was very hungry. He hoped that Felicity hadn't waited for him, because Felicity hungry as well as angry might need more attention than he really wanted to devote to her just now.

Bless her!

He went in, and a gray-haired porter's eyes lit up.

"Back again, Mr. Dawlish."

"That's right, you can't keep a hungry man from his

luncheon for long. Do you know if my wife is in the dining room?"

"Well, no, she isn't," the porter said, and the light faded from his eyes, bewilderment replacing it. "I didn't give her your message personally, she wasn't in her room when I rang. Dr. Miller took it to her, as he was going along. I must admit that I was surprised when she left soon afterward."

Suddenly Dawlish felt himself grow cold.

"So she did leave."

"Oh, yes, sir, only a few minutes after your call. She was obviously going for a swim. I was on the telephone, but I saw that she was dressed in her beach wrap and swimsuit."

"What time?" asked Dawlish abruptly, and then realized that he could answer for himself, for he had telephoned about twenty past one. "Never mind, thanks. If she comes back, ask her not to set foot outside the hotel. Make sure you give her that message in person." He turned toward the door, and hesitated. "Who is Dr. Miller?"

"He's one of the guests, sir. His room was next to the one which Mrs. Dawlish was using."

"I see," said Dawlish, and asked almost tensely: "Do you know where he is now?"

"He drove away about half an hour ago."

"Is he coming back?"

"I don't think so, sir, he was only due to stay until midday. Been here since Saturday, sir."

"What was he like to look at?" Dawlish produced a pound note, encouragingly.

"Well, sir, a very well-spoken gentleman, extremely well-dressed, about thirty-five or so. Dark and good-looking, sir. Is that enough?"

Dawlish said quietly, "Anything that might be called a distinguishing feature?"

"Well, sir—in a way. He had a black eye."

"Good lord! A fresh one?"

"Fairly recent, I imagine, sir."

38

"Thanks." Dawlish summoned a smile as he turned and went out through the swing doors, which the small boy had now completely forgotten.

Again, the sun blasted Dawlish.

The reflection from the water dazzled him.

He could see no one who looked remotely like Felicity in the water, or on the beach, or coming toward him. He felt that he wanted to be in several places at once, but first he had to make sure that Felicity wasn't out there. So he went closer to the beach, and stood gripping the hot railings and staring at each bather in turn.

Felicity was not there.

Way out, close to the horizon and almost lost to sight, was a small boat; he saw that without giving it a second thought.

Felicity had gone to bathe, and had not come back.

She could not have gotten his message, or she would not have gone.

Next to Felicity, he wanted to find this Dr. Miller with the black eye.

6 SEARCH

THE SEA WAS EVEN more like glass.

Close to the beach there was a faint ripple, but that was all. There was no sound here, now, and even about the girders of the pier there was no movement. The hush over the sea seemed to have affected the people on the beach, for many were eating, sitting in groups of deck chairs, and many were lying back, with newspapers over their faces. A few were lying on their faces or their backs, every possible inch of flesh exposed. Nothing was more typical of a British seaside resort than this; even to the boy, trudging with a box hanging from his neck and calling:

". . . cream ices . . . cream ices . . ." and even to the children going up to him, with coppers or silver held out trustingly. Near Dawlish, two girls in swimsuits stopped to stare at him, but theirs was genuine admiration for a remarkable-looking man.

No; there was no sign of Felicity.

Dawlish seemed to unlock his mind. He could go back to the hotel and ask more questions, particularly about the man named Miller, but the vital thing was to make sure that Felicity was not here.

Could anyone drown in such a sea as this?

He eased his grip on the railing, and as he did so, a man approached from behind him.

"Excuse me, Mr. Dawlish."

Dawlish swung around. "Yes?"

It was one of the policemen; and not far along a police car had drawn up, with a driver at the wheel. This man saw Dawlish's expression, and was completely taken aback. Dawlish, bleak-eyed, saw that but could not make himself relax.

"Er—sorry to worry you, sir, but I thought you would like to know about the driver of the sports car."

"I—yes, thanks." Any news might help.

"He's driven out of town, sir, heading for London."

That was no help at all.

"I see, thanks."

"Is anything the matter, sir?"

Dawlish said slowly, heavily: "Yes. I haven't time to explain, but very simply it's this: my wife came here to bathe half an hour or so ago. She hasn't come back and she doesn't seem to be in the water, now."

The policeman exclaimed, "On a day like *this?*"

"On a day like this. Will you——"

"I'll make some inquiries at once," the policeman promised. "The beach attendant for this section is over there; I'll

40

get him. One or two of the promettes might be helpful, too, there isn't much they miss. What time was it?"

"About half an hour ago."

"Can you give me a brief description of Mrs. Dawlish, sir?"

Dawlish was both brief and vivid. . . .

He was as much on edge as he had ever been in his life, but he had to admire the speed with which the search was organized. A few words passed between the policeman and a beach attendant in a dark blue swimsuit, and this man summoned several of the promenade information girls—the promettes. Others were called in; so were the deck chair attendants and boatmen. Word spread, as if like fire. Men and girls started to question the people on the beach, and party after party was interrogated.

The questions were all the same.

Had anyone seemed to be in trouble out at sea?

No.

No, no, no, no.

Time and time again Dawlish heard a man or woman say that he'd seen Felicity go out, a tall, slim woman wearing a golden-colored swimsuit, a one-piece; and a shiny gilt bathing cap. There wasn't any doubt that she had come this way. Two youngish men could give details. They had seen her hurry from the promenade, drop her wrap close to the wall, and go straight into the water; she had hardly stopped. A policeman went for the wrap and brought it back. Dawlish identified it beyond doubt.

There was nothing else at all.

Had anyone seen her come back?

No.

No, no, no, no.

The two young men remembered her swimming some distance out. She had given them the impression that she was a strong swimmer. It was obvious that as soon as she had

41

stopped being a woman with a fine, smooth body, and had become head and arms in the water, their interest had faded. Why not? A small boy seemed to remember that she had gone under the pier.

No one had seen her come out.

"Of course, there was quite a tide," one of the beach attendants said. "Quite strong, out beneath the pier. She could have been carried through the pier and gone back the other side. It's not likely, but we ought to make inquiries over that way."

They hurried to the other side of the pier.

No one had seen Felicity.

"I can't believe that anything serious would happen to her if she was such a strong swimmer, sir," the policeman said. "Not on a day like this."

Dawlish hardly answered.

"We'll keep the closest watch," the man promised.

"I'm sure you will. Thanks," said Dawlish.

The shock of the disappearance was greater than he had realized; he could not think clearly, was not even sure that he was doing the right thing. He went back, alone, to the hotel. There was the porter, the doorboy and the elderly head porter, all quite normal, unaware of any trouble. Then they saw Dawlish's expression and became fully aware of it.

"Is everything all right, sir?" That was the head porter.

"My wife hasn't come back, and she's not in the water."

"*What*, sir?"

The other porter said, like an echo, "On a day like this . . ."

"That's right," Dawlish said, and stopped himself from barking at the man. "Did anyone watch her as she left?"

"Well, sir, we were all pretty busy," the head porter replied. "I'll inquire among the taxi men outside, it's just possible that they noticed something."

He hurried outside.

It would be a pointless quest, Dawlish knew. No one could have any doubt as to the fact that Felicity had actually gone straight from the hotel into the sea. It was the fact that she hadn't come back that mattered. He could imagine a watch being kept all along the beach—a watch for a body which had been washed ashore. He could not believe that it had happened, and yet the fear struck deeply into him. He had known danger for Felicity before. She had disappeared before. There had been one time in America when . . .

Never mind the past!

His head ached, badly. He realized that he was hungry, and yet didn't feel that he could eat. He could do with a drink, though, his mouth was parched. He went further into the lounge and a waiter came up.

"Can I get you anything, sir?"

"Are beer and sandwiches possible?"

"Quite possible, sir. What sort of sandwiches?"

"Meaty." Dawlish waved his hands, and tried to behave as if his whole being wasn't in torment, but it was. The sun and the sea and the people enjoying themselves so gaily all mocked him. The people having their after-lunch snoozes. An elderly man snoring, in a corner. A woman stroking the back of a pug-nosed pomeranian, as if nothing else in the world deserved such affection. Life was normal, the world was happy, and Felicity had run into the sea and had not come back.

The elderly head porter came, slowly; obviously he had no news.

"The taxi men didn't notice anything unusual, sir. I suppose you're quite sure that Mrs. Dawlish did go into the sea?"

"Positive."

"Well, sir, there's just one possibility that I haven't tried," said the porter. "Old Mr. Harrison usually sits at his window while he's having his lunch—he's an old resident, goes about in a wheel chair and has all his meals in his room. It wouldn't be the first time that he'd seen something which others hadn't noticed. Twice last year he raised several alarms when swimmers were in danger, but that wasn't on a day like this. I'll send up and ask him, if you like."

"May I go and see him?"

"Well—I'll telephone and ask him if he'll see you, sir."

"Thanks," said Dawlish. "Hurry, will you?"

The waiter arrived with beer and sandwiches, and put them on a small table near the hall. Dawlish began to drink as he watched the porter's desk. The old man seemed to be a long time on the telephone, and when he had finished three hotel guests came up with queries. Dawlish made himself sit there and eat, although the sandwiches, succulent though they were, almost choked him.

At last, the porter came across.

"Mr. Harrison will be happy to see you, sir. It's room 501—the liftman will direct you."

"Fine," said Dawlish. "Thanks."

A lift was waiting. The one-armed attendant was not over garrulous, nor was he particularly curious. Dawlish reached the fifth floor and turned right, as directed. Room 501 was only a short distance from the lift. He tapped, and after a moment's pause the door opened and a man in a wheel chair looked up at him; a man who looked as if he were nearer eighty than seventy, whose pale, watery old eyes could not have seen anything; it was just another waste of time.

"Mr. Dawlish?" The voice was unexpectedly deep and steady, nothing like so old as the wizened face. "Come in, come in, sir. I didn't understand what that fool of a porter was saying. Something about a missing swimmer, is that it?"

"Yes, my wife, Mr. Harrison."

"Oh, indeed. Missing?"

"She was seen to enter the water, but not to come out."

"Oh, really? Your wife, eh? What time was this?"

"About one-fifteen."

"I see, one-fifteen." The old man turned his chair and sped toward the window on the other side of the large room, which must have had the best position in Brighton. The sun on the water was bright, but this room was cool even at this time of the day, because of awnings at the window. "Let me see, now. Tall lady?"

Anyone's guess.

"Yes, about five feet eight."

"Odd thing, to get lost on a day like this," Harrison remarked.

If anyone else used that phrase, Dawlish thought, he would scream. But the old man's eyes seemed to be scanning the water keenly enough, and if he had been sitting here at the time, he must have seen Felicity go in; he could see most of the beach and all of the pier.

"Dressed in a yellow swimsuit?"

Dawlish's heart leapt. "Yes!"

"Tall, slender, nice figure," said the old man, and he turned to look at Dawlish. "With friends?"

"No, she was alone."

"Nonsense," said Mr. Harrison.

"I understand that she was alone," Dawlish said carefully.

"Mistaken," said Harrison, and his eyes opened very wide. "Wives do peculiar things when the husbands aren't looking. No need to tell you that, you look as if you're a man of the world. She was with friends."

Dawlish didn't argue, but felt his heart beating faster, realized that this frail old man was his one reason to hope. And Harrison seemed to be so sure of himself.

"Well, she may have met someone she knew."

"In a motorboat."

"*What?*"

"I'm trying to tell you what happened, don't keep interrupting," the old man said, almost crossly. "She was swimming out there, very good swimmer, couldn't mistake her yellow suit. Played around near the pier. Then her friends arrived, and took the boat alongside. Couldn't see what happened under the pier, but next time I saw her she was on board with them."

Dawlish felt as if he was choking.

"Did you see which way they went?"

"Shoreham way," answered Harrison. "I couldn't keep them in sight long, from this window." He waved vaguely, obviously not realizing that he was taking in the whole of the English Channel. "Out that way, somewhere. A motor-boat."

"How far out were they?"

"Near the end of the pier."

"Did you notice how many people were in the boat?"

"Man and woman." Harrison gave a little cackle of a laugh, which came out quite unexpectedly. "No doubt about that, Mr. Dawlish, man *and* a woman. Dark-haired man, woman in a red cap, big-breasted I'd say. That's all I can tell you."

"Would you recognize the boat again?"

"Don't know about that, but I'd recognize the kind of boat," Harrison said. "One of Old Kerry's. He hires them out by the hour or the day. They always come back, too," he added dryly.

Dawlish said, "I'm in a tearing hurry now, Mr. Harrison, but before long I'll come back and tell you how very grateful I am." He gave Harrison a smile which seemed to gratify even old age, and turned and almost ran out of the room.

7 INVITATION

"AYE, SIR, 'TIS TRUE, SIR," said the man named Old Kerry. He was, in fact, very little younger than Harrison, and he sat on the upturned keel of a dinghy which obviously needed

46

caulking, pulling at a pipe, peaked cap jaunty at the side of his head, old gray-blue sweater, weathered by many years, high up to the neck in spite of the afternoon warmth. "Hired 'un out, I did."

Old Kerry was a character, and meant to remain a character for as long as he could. His speech was slow and deliberately overdone, and there was a contemplative air about him as he looked Dawlish up and down.

Dawlish was alone.

"Had 'un the whole day they did, and paid me ten pounds as a deposit, which is fair enough. Ain't known anyone run away with one of me boats yet, it'll be back."

"How much petrol did they have on board?"

"Full tank and a spare can, sir."

"How far would it take them?"

"French coast and back, if that's where they wanted to go." Old Kerry took his pipe from his mouth and went on: "That's the way they be heading when I last saw them, too." He pointed with the pipe. "That direction, sir."

"Thanks," said Dawlish, and played his pound note trick. "Had you ever seen them before?"

"No, sir, I never did, and I've a good memory for faces. You need it on a job like this," the old man added reflectively.

"I'm sure you do," said Dawlish. He slipped the pound into an old but capable hand, forced a smile, and turned away. "Thanks, Mr. Kerry." He walked over the big stones and pebbles toward the nearest steps up to the promenade, and found it heavy going; he seemed to sink down more on one side than another. Children were playing, bathing, singing, crying; parents were sleeping, snoring, talking, reading, remonstrating. There was a queue a dozen strong for rowboats.

Dawlish reached the steps and hurried up them, but did not quite know why he was hurrying. He faced the facts. Felicity had been taken aboard a hired motorboat, which had headed out for the coast of France, or in that general direction. She had not gone willingly; that was unthinkable. Old Harrison's eyes had missed what had happened beneath the pier.

Dawlish drew close to the hotel.

He was not quite sure what to do next. It was possible that the doctor named Miller, who had given Felicity the message, could have something to do with it. It was just possible that Felicity had received the message but, still being annoyed, had decided to ignore it. In some moods Felicity would do just that.

Dawlish didn't really think it likely.

He reached the hotel.

By now, he felt sure that life was almost normal on the beach; the police had discovered nothing, and except that there would be a lookout for the body, nothing else would be done. All the policemen concerned would be sorry for him, but that was all; and dead bathers were taken out of the water too often to distress them too much.

Should he tell them about the motorboat?

He tried to fit that into the pieces of the puzzle as he knew it, but it wasn't easy. One thing was. Old Harrison had an eye for a figure, too, and there was no doubt that the couple who had hired the boat and had taken Felicity out of the water were the Bikini Blonde and her sallow-faced companion.

He, Dawlish, had been taken for a ride.

What could he do?

What could the police do?

They could trace this Dr. Miller much more quickly than he, for one thing. They could trace the sports car with help from London, too. By himself, he could do practically nothing.

The porter on duty outside looked at him worriedly; so did the taxi drivers. So did the doorboy. But there was eagerness in the elderly porter's eyes as he called out to Dawlish from the porter's desk:

"Mr. Dawlish, sir!"

Dawlish hurried.

"There's a telephone message for you, sir—will you call a Hove number?"

"Who was the message from?"

"I'm afraid I don't know, sir, but it was a lady." He handed Dawlish a slip of paper with a number written on it. "Would you like to make the call from the prepayment box, sir? I have some coppers if you haven't."

"I've plenty, thanks," Dawlish said.

The telephone cubicles were in the corner opposite; and each was empty. He squeezed himself inside, could hardly drop the coins into the box quickly enough, and he had to steel himself to dial the numbers without getting them mixed. Then came the inevitable ringing sound, and although it lasted for only a few seconds, it seemed an age. He found himself wondering where the call was, and whether he should have gone to the police after all.

All this time the number was ringing, brrr-brrr; brrr-brrr.

It stopped.

" 'Allo," a man said.

That 'allo was a mine of information. No Englishman could ever speak like it, there was only one race in the world which said 'allo in quite the same way on the telephone: the French.

"Patrick Dawlish speaking," said Dawlish very slowly, and now his voice was quite steady.

"That is Mr. Patrick Dawlish?"

"Yes, speaking."

"Thank you, sir. I have a message for you, if you please."

"What is the message?"

"You do not need to worry, Mr. Dawlish. Please wait quietly at home, and you will receive further information."

49

"What is your name?" Dawlish asked, and only just stopped himself from crying: "Where is my wife? I want to see you."

"Good-bye," the Frenchman said, and rang off.

Dawlish replaced the receiver very slowly. He looked straight across the hall at the elderly porter, now attending to a big man who had just come in. This man turned suddenly, and looked straight into Dawlish's eyes. He was dressed in a dark brown suit, not particularly well cut, there was a heavy look about him, and his perspiring forehead showed a dark red ridge where the brim of his hat had pressed too tightly. He was no holiday-maker, no tourist; he was much more likely a plainclothes detective.

Dawlish pushed open the door and stepped out. The other man came forward promptly.

"Mr. Patrick Dawlish?"

"Yes. Good afternoon."

"Good afternoon, sir." The man held out a card. "I'm Detective Inspector Greenstreet, of the Brighton Criminal Investigation Department."

"Ah, yes."

"Can you spare me five minutes, please?"

"Yes," said Dawlish, and led the way, had he but known it, to the corner where Felicity had had her drink that morning. "Too late for a drink and too early for tea, I'm afraid," he said. "Care for a lemon squash?"

"No thanks, sir." Greenstreet was a little too large for the wicker armchair into which he lowered himself. He had brown eyes, brown hair and a brown skin; so dark that he might be slightly colored. His eyes were very direct, and he was probably in his late thirties. "I've been studying certain reports, sir, and I am given to understand . . ."

Dawlish kept thinking of the French voice and its cryptic message; and of Felicity. Through all that, one thing penetrated. It would be easy to underestimate the Brighton Police. They knew all that there was to know. They had talked to Old Kerry and Old Harrison, they had even found the boy who had brought the suitcase to Felicity. Greenstreet made all this clear, in an unexpected tenor voice, and then went on:

"My instructions are to inquire exactly what is happening, Mr. Dawlish, and to ask you to be quite frank."

"Naturally," Dawlish said. "That isn't difficult." He weighed his words, and weighed his decision, and reached it while he was speaking; he hoped that he was doing the right thing. "I had a message last night, from a man representing himself to be M. Jules Bidot. . . ."

He told everything, even including the message from the man whom he had just telephoned.

Greenstreet looked fully satisfied.

"And what number was it, sir?"

Dawlish handed him the slip.

"I'll trace this call," said Greenstreet. "Will you be here for the next hour?"

"As far as I know."

"If you decide to leave, have a message sent to the police station at once, please," Greenstreet said, and hurried out, big and burly and likely soon to be much too hot. Dawlish watched him go, and then turned and went along to the room where Felicity had changed.

There was her soft, mauve suit, of silk; her gloves, stockings, girdle and bra, her little mauve hat. There was the ghost of Felicity, who had set out this morning so eager and so anxious to meet Mme. Bidot.

And that telephone call had been a hoax, unless . . .

Bidot had been prevented from coming.

Dawlish picked up a nylon stocking and drew it gently over his hand. It was soft as gossamer, and very long. He drew it over his hand again, seeing Felicity in his mind's eye. He knew of no reason in the world why Felicity should have been kidnapped. He could only think that it was to exert pressure on him, but he did not know who might be behind it. The only obvious possibility was that it was concerned with Bidot's call.

There was only one thing to do.

Find Bidot; find out why he hadn't arrived here, and then find out if he had in fact telephoned last night, from London.

If ever there was a case in which the police could help, this was it. The Brighton men would gladly try, but in London there was Superintendent Trivett, one of the senior men at Scotland Yard, a friend of Dawlish, and a friend of Felicity.

Dawlish lifted the telephone.

In his office at Scotland Yard, Superintendent Trivett sweltered, and fumed, for it was not easy to forget that it was Bank Holiday. He was wishing himself on the river when he received the call from Dawlish, listened, and promptly said:

"I'll see if I can find Bidot, Pat."

"Make it a quickie, will you?" said Dawlish. "I'll be at your office about five."

"What are you going to do, fly?" Trivett demanded. "You be careful, with the traffic on the road today you could pile yourself up."

"Five past five," amended Dawlish, and rang off.

Trivett smiled a little grimly as he replaced the receiver, dabbed his forehead and then lifted the receiver again and spoke to a Chief Inspector whose duty it was to know all that was going on in the hotels of London, and who was acquainted with most of the millionaires, politicians, film stars and lesser celebrities in the West End.

"He was staying at the Savoy," the C.I. said. "His wife held a press conference yesterday. I'll call you back."

"Make it as quick as you can. Haven't heard that Bidot's in any kind of trouble, have you?"

"No. He's adept in keeping out of it. Why?"

"Dawlish is interested in him."

"Oh, *is* he," said the C.I. heavily. "Then Bidot's probably in a lot more trouble than he realized. I'll find out all I can, sir. So long."

8 FACTS ABOUT BIDOT

DAWLISH WAS AHEAD of the homeward rush of traffic. Even the wisest of the day trippers and weekenders were lured by the sun to stay late at the beach, and at four o'clock there was very little on the road in either direction. Dawlish restrained his urge for speed until he was out of the thirty-mile-an-hour area, and then put his foot down. The London to Brighton road is good most of the way, its only trouble being that it was made to carry only about a quarter of the traffic imposed upon it.

Dawlish really drove fast.

Occasionally people turned to stare. Most of the time, they took no notice. It was twenty minutes to five when he reached the first of the outer London suburbs, and was forced to slow down, but even here the traffic was light and policemen few, and he took chances which normally he would not have taken. He reached Westminster Bridge as Big Ben was striking five, and swung into the gateway of New Scotland Yard one minute later. Few Flying Squad cars turned in so swiftly, and a policeman on duty near the steps skipped out of the way.

"Sorry to wake you," Dawlish said politely, getting out and slamming the door. He beamed. "Hi," he said, and strode toward the flight of stone steps which led to the Criminal Investigation building.

Only one thing new had been added since he had left Brighton.

He had not been followed.

As far as he could judge, no one had taken the slightest interest in him.

He was welcomed like an old friend by the sergeant on duty in the hall, and told to go straight up to Mr. Trivett, who was expecting him. Trivett would not let him down. Dawlish reached the lift, was greeted as by another old friend, the liftman, and before he reached Trivett's office had spoken to eight men and one stenographer. He tapped at Trivett's door, and Trivett called at once:

"Come in."

It was a large office, with two desks, one larger than the other. Trivett was standing up from the larger. Big, wide windows overlooked the Embankment, and traffic noises were coming in a variety of tones. The breeze was fluttering the leaves of the plane trees which grew close to the window.

Trivett was smiling, but he looked warm and not particularly cheerful. He was a tall, good-looking man, very broad across the shoulders, and in recent years running slightly to fat around the middle. These two men had been friends for twenty years and understood each other as only close friends could.

"Well, Bill," said Dawlish. "Traced Bidot?"

"Yes," said Trivett. "He flew back to Paris early this afternoon. Wouldn't like to tell me what it's all about, would you?"

Dawlish didn't answer at once.

He sat looking as if intently at Trivett but it was obvious that he was hardly aware of the Yard man. His expression was bleak and his lips set tightly. His blue eyes were narrowed, and they seemed to glint. He was a giant in a strange kind of stillness, and it was possible to imagine great storms raging inside him.

Trivett had never seen him look quite like this.

Very slowly, Dawlish moved. Trivett saw that he was

groping for his cigarettes, but did nothing to interrupt. Dawlish took out his case, a cigarette, a lighter; he lit up with the same slow deliberation.

"So he was here, and was frightened off," he said very softly. "I wonder how they frightened him. Did you get any information about his wife?"

"You didn't ask anything about his wife."

"That's right," said Dawlish. "But I'm asking now. Bill, Felicity was taken away this morning under my very nose. The obvious reason is to exert some kind of pressure on me. I don't know more than that. Brighton has all the details, don't ask me to give them to you, there's a good chap. How long will it take you to find out where Mme. Bidot is?"

Trivett said huskily: "Fel snatched?" It was at least ten seconds before he stretched out for the telephone. "Put me through to Chief Inspector Warren," he said, and held on only for a moment, while Dawlish, drawing very deeply on his cigarette, stood up and went to the window and looked on to the sunlit Embankment scene. "Hallo, Warren," Trivett went on, and Dawlish continued to stare out of the window. "When you checked on Bidot, did you find out anything about his wife? . . . Yes, I see . . . Yes. . . ."

Dawlish turned to stare at him.

Trivett made one or two scratchy notes with a pencil, and then said, "I'll let you know if I want anything more, thanks." He rang off. "Bidot went home by himself," he said. "Warren took it for granted that Mme. Bidot was still at the Savoy, but she isn't. She left this morning, with a family friend named Maidment. Anything odd about that?"

Dawlish looked at him squarely.

"No," he said slowly, "I suppose there isn't. Husband and wife don't have to live in each other's pockets, do they? Thanks, Bill." He moved toward the door and gave his bleakest smile yet. "I'll be seeing you."

Trivett sprang up.

"Not so fast! If we're to help find Felicity——"

"Don't even try," said Dawlish. "Not yet, anyhow. I don't like the way this is shaping at all, Bill. My job." He raised a hand in a kind of mock salute, and went out moving with hardly a sound, closing the door gently behind him. Trivett did not follow, but went straight to the telephone, lifted it, called Warren again, and said:

"I want you to get everything you can on the Bidots. Whom they've seen while they've been over here, where they've been, anything that might be useful if we have to put out a call for them in a hurry. We may have to. Right, thanks." He rang off, but didn't lift his hand from the telephone, and when he spoke into it again, he said to the operator, "Get me the Duty Superintendent at Brighton, at once."

Then Trivett rang off.

Dawlish stepped into the shadowy coolness of the courtyard. The big C.I.D. building hid most of the sun, and here it was in shadow, while just across the water the County Hall and the hospital were bright in the sun. The water shimmered, glass-like, as the sea had at Brighton. He nodded to the various men who greeted him, got into the Allard, and drove out much more cautiously than he had driven in. Traffic was still very light. He did not go far, just along Whitehall, across St. James's Park and into the heart of Mayfair. Here, too, London seemed to have been deserted, and there was a kind of blight upon the earth. Yet children and dogs played in the spacious squares, and those who walked looked warm and red. The parks themselves were crowded with people who all seemed busy.

Dawlish came to a small mews leading off one of the squares, and pulled up outside a doorway at the head of a flight of cement steps. He ran up these, and rang the bell.

At first, there was no answer.

"Out for the day," he said *sotto voce*, and rang again. "They don't usually——"

He heard footsteps.

He glanced toward the square, and made sure that no one was watching him; he felt sure that no one had followed. He turned back to the door as it opened, and a pleasant-looking, suntanned woman in her late thirties stood there, fresh and attractive, and obviously glad to see him.

"Why, Pat!"

"Hallo, Joan," said Dawlish. "I hoped you wouldn't be at the Hyde Park Lido." He took her hands and kissed her lightly on the cheek. "You look wonderful."

"Where's Fel?"

"Er—gone swimming. Ted in?"

"Yes, in the garden. Tim's here, too."

"Sometimes Fate is kind," said Dawlish as he stepped inside. Joan Beresford, wife of his closest friend, and lifelong intimate of Felicity, frowned as he did so, as if his mood had already passed itself on to her.

"I'd just come in to mix some drinks," Joan said.

"There couldn't be a better idea," applauded Dawlish, and then they reached the small kitchen of the little mews house, and he smiled down on her, but without the familiar glint in his eyes. "Joan, you're going to hate me, but I'm going to take the risk. Fel's missing. I don't know what it's about, but I've never needed help more than I do now. Don't give Ted hell if I persuade him to lend a hand, will you?"

"Felicity *missing!*" Joan echoed, as if the very idea seemed fantastic.

Dawlish nodded mutely.

"If there's any way I can help, too, make sure that I know," Joan said, with swift and absolute understanding.

Dawlish squeezed her arm before going to the little flight of steps leading down to a tiny walled garden. This was almost a miracle in the heart of London; there should have been no garden here at all, for tall houses surrounded the mews. But in the middle was a small patch of bright green

57

lawn, tended by Joan as carefully as her own hair. Three borders looked as if every flower known to England's summer was there in full bloom. Deck chairs were on the lawn, a small table, books and newspapers. Sprawled back on one chair was a tall, thin man, and sitting in an upright chair with wooden arms was a much heavier man, with dark hair turning gray at the sides, and a face which some regarded as ugly and all as homely; but could at times be remarkably attractive.

This was Ted Beresford.

The other man was Timothy Jeremy.

Neither of them had yet seen Dawlish, who went down the steps very quietly. Tim was pretending to read, but now and again he looked up from his book and stared at the flowers; it was doubtful whether he knew what he was doing. Tim was having wife trouble; and serious trouble at that. For years, he and his wife had not gotten on too well, and recently she had fallen in love with a younger man. The divorce would be absolute in a few days' time.

Dawlish reached the foot of the steps, and then inquired mildly:

"Either of you like a piece o' cake?"

It was a sign of Tim Jeremy's taut nerves that he actually jumped; a sign of Ted Beresford's steady ones that he did not even turn his head. Tim not only jumped but scrambled out of his chair.

"Pat!"

"Hallo, Tim," Dawlish said. "Big slice of cake, too."

"Just offer it to me again," Jeremy said.

"Now what's all this?" Beresford turned at last, and looked Dawlish up and down; few men could appear more ungainly than Ted, and the waistband of his trousers was loosened at the top two buttons for comfort's sake when sitting.

Dawlish told them, and they became taut with anxiety and with eagerness to help.

Joan came out with the drinks.

They talked and made plans for twenty minutes, and at the end of that time Dawlish said very quietly:

"That's fine. One day I'll really be able to say thanks. Ted, you'll go with Joan to Paris then, and on the first available plane, and see what you can find out about Bidot. Keep away from the police, except in real emergency. Stay at the usual place near St. Germain des Prés if you can, and if not, leave a message for us there," Dawlish went on. "Tim, you go down to Alum village, but don't go to the house. There's the gamekeeper's hut near the orchard—if there's a message or need to make contact, leave a message or telephone me when I get there."

"Expect trouble there?" Tim asked.

"Just want to be ready in case there is," Dawlish said. "Now I'm going to the Savoy, and after that, home."

"Give me a reasonable start," said Tim Jeremy, whose brooding and unhappy look had been vanquished by eagerness.

"There's one thing you haven't explained," Joan said, quietly. "Where do you think Mme. Bidot has gone?"

Dawlish said: "I'm guessing, Joan, but I suspect that Bidot was going to ask me to take on some job for him—one on which he didn't want to call in the police. Before he could get to Brighton he was scared off. His wife left the Savoy this morning, unexpectedly, and it's at least possible that the same trick was played with her as with Felicity."

"I see," said Joan.

"And you really haven't the faintest idea what it's all about?" asked Tim.

"All I know is that if I can't find an angle to work soon, I'll go crazy," Dawlish said.

He did not look crazy when he stepped into the Savoy Hotel. He looked cool, fresh and gigantic. The porters and the reception staff knew him well, and were at pains to acknowledge him. He strolled across to reception, where an elderly man with whom he always dealt when booking friends in stood waiting to serve.

"And where will your friends come from this time, Mr. Dawlish? The United States, Australia, Singapore or——"

"I'm looking for someone who's already been here," Dawlish said, quite amicably and mildly. "You've probably heard of Mme. Bidot."

The elderly man broke into a laugh, which was one of the things which were not done in that hotel at that particular spot, and he choked the laugh back immediately. But he was smiling.

"It is like asking if I have heard of Marilyn Monroe."

"Is she really as lovely as they say?"

"Mr. Dawlish, I think she is the most beautiful woman I have ever seen."

"Coming from you, that's something," said Dawlish. "She left this morning, didn't she?"

"Yes."

"About what time?"

"It would be a little after ten o'clock, sir."

"Was M. Bidot here then?"

"No," said the elderly receptionist reflectively. "M. Bidot left the hotel a little before nine o'clock this morning, in his hired Rolls-Royce. It was while he was away that Mme. Bidot left."

"Did he seem surprised that she'd gone?"

The receptionist hesitated, and glanced around, as if he was nervous in case these questions and his answers were being overheard. He looked rather worried and even more elderly now; and undoubtedly that was concerned with the fact that he knew much about Dawlish's reputation.

"Is there trouble of any kind, Mr. Dawlish?"

"Yes," said Dawlish flatly. "Big trouble."

"Well, sir, in the strictest confidence—when M. Bidot came back, he looked positively ill. Never seen such a change in a man. He is a very charming gentleman, most popular whenever he stayed here—in fact both he and Mme. Bidot were popular. Several of us noticed the change in him, and as Mme. Bidot had left with her luggage—well, we rather drew our own conclusions, sir."

"That there was a rift in the marital lute," observed Dawlish. "Did Mme. Bidot leave by herself?"

"Well——"

"You know, I wouldn't ask all this if it wasn't essential that I should know."

"I quite understand, sir," the receptionist said. "As a matter of fact, she left with a Dr. Maidment, whom I understood was a family friend."

"Maidment," Dawlish echoed; and his thoughts flew back to the elderly porter at Brighton, who had asked Dr. Miller to give Felicity his, Dawlish's, message. He guessed hopefully. "Did this Dr. Maidment have a black eye?"

"Well I never!" the man exclaimed, and looked at Dawlish with amazement. "So he had!"

"Was he well-dressed, dark, thirty-five or so?"

"Obviously you know him," the receptionist said.

"Above everything else in the world, I need to know where to find this Dr. Maidment," Dawlish said, very slowly. "Do you know where he lives?"

"As a matter of fact, I don't, sir. He has never stayed here although he has been in several times. He had dinner with M'sieur and Madame on Thursday night. He is Dr. Claude Maidment, I do know that. It is just possible that one of the porters knows where he lives, he may have taken a taxi from here. Shall I inquire?"

"Just as fast as you can."

"If you'll take a seat, sir, I'll see what I can do."

Dawlish said, "Let me have a telephone directory, will you?"

"Yes, sir."

Dawlish found only one Dr. C. Maidment, and went to a telephone and called the number. The doctor himself answered, and took only seconds to establish that he wasn't Dr. Maidment *alias* Dr. Miller.

Dawlish rang off, still in a fever of anxiety, which he had to fight back.

Soon, the receptionist came back.

"Any luck?" Dawlish demanded almost too eagerly.

"As a matter of fact, sir, yes and no. Dr. Maidment and Mme. Bidot left in Dr. Maidment's car, which was chauffeur-driven, and the chauffeur happened to mention that he was heading south. Does that help?"

"No," said Dawlish slowly. "I don't see that it does. Did you find out if our Dr. Maidment has a London address?"

"None that is known to us, sir."

"All right," said Dawlish, and summoned a smile, and slipped a note into the other's hand. "Keep trying to find out where he lives, will you? I'd like to know everything I can about this Dr. Maidment and the Bidots. And don't be too surprised if the police start inquiring soon."

"If they do, we shall have to tell them everything we know, sir."

"I wouldn't dream of suggesting that you keep anything back, except possibly the fact that I've been asking questions ahead of them," said Dawlish. "We don't want to touch them on their vanity, do we?" He kept a poker face as he turned away.

The receptionist was smiling, a little uneasily.

Dawlish climbed to the wheel of his car, started off, and felt as if the whole sunlit evening was one of darkness and dismay. It was now nearly seven o'clock, and six hours had passed since Felicity had disappeared. He didn't like the thoroughness with which all this had been planned. This Dr. Maidment, if Maidment was his real name, had him where he wanted him; and he seemed to have Bidot in the same corner, presumably for the same reason.

It wasn't good to realize.

9 WELCOME HOME

DAWLISH WAS DESPERATELY ANXIOUS for action; the fact that there was nothing he could do made the situation unbearable. Any kind of action, almost any kind of movement, would help to throw off the worst of the depression which had settled on him. Through the suburbs of London he battled with traffic, and he longed for the open road. It wasn't far to Haslemere, where he lived; but Haslemere was on a main highway to the south coast, and as soon as he left the metropolis he ran into the homecoming traffic, stretching bumper to bumper. Big cars and little cars, huge buses and small coaches, motorcyclists and pedal cyclists came along in their tens of thousands, their one thought to get home.

There was only a trickle of traffic heading south, with Dawlish. But every driver who dared swung out to pass the long line of traffic, and every hundred yards had its dangers and its moments of madness. Gritting his teeth, glaring at every man who swung out and thus slowed him down, and almost choked with petrol fumes, Dawlish drove on. Not until he reached Guildford was he able to get off the main road, on to by-roads. These were not so busy, but neither were they so empty as he had known them, and they twisted and turned, up and down hill.

It was a nightmare journey, and in all took him an hour and a half.

At last, he came within sight of his house.

This stood on a slight rise in the land, back from the road. It had a large garden, and there were apple trees and pear trees in abundance and even pigs, for at one time he had hoped to keep pigs on a farming scale. He had long since dropped that idea, but the orchards gave him a hobby, and the pigs bacon. The house was in mock Tudor style, built between the wars by a good builder with first-class materials. It was bordered on one side by extensive meadowland and on another by trees where the gamekeeper's hut was, and there were many acres of open moorland nearby. Beyond the house, perhaps two miles away, was the little village of Alum, and beyond Alum, Haslemere itself. This was one of the loveliest parts of Surrey, and so secluded that few people passed by chance. Today, a few motorists trying to avoid the main highways and a few cyclists were on the narrow road, but no one got in Dawlish's way.

He slowed down to turn into the driveway, which was steep and narrow, with grassy banks on either side. He changed gear, and swung around. He looked right and left, but saw only the trees on the banks, the trim grass which he himself had cut with a power mower only the evening before. Then Felicity had trimmed the edges of the grass and the beds around the trees. She had worn an old brown sun dress and had her hair untidy; yesterday had been a golden, lazy day.

Dawlish pulled up at the circular drive in front of the house. This drive led on the one side to the garage and the outhouses, and small vans could be driven down to the orchard. No one was in sight, and he expected no one, for the staff were off for the weekend. He had assumed that he would be back in time to feed the pigs and the two dogs and Felicity's cat.

No dogs came bounding.

Dawlish stepped out of the Allard and looked at the house. Again, his heart began to pound. With its leaded glass windows, its gables and its oak beams, it looked as if it had been standing there for a century or more, instead of twenty short years. But Dawlish wasn't interested in the house itself.

The windows were open.

He could almost hear Felicity calling to him, as he had come from the front door:

"Did you shut the kitchen window, darling?"

He hadn't. He'd gone back and shut it. He'd checked these front-room windows, and there was no doubt that he had left them securely fastened. Now they were open, and the evening sun shone upon them.

Could Fel be back?

He sprang up the steps leading to the front door, but saw no one. He was in a state of absolute confusion, because of the possibility that this had been a gigantic hoax, that Felicity would be waiting for him; perhaps getting supper, or pouring a drink, or at her never-ending tapestries.

The front door was ajar.

If it wasn't Felicity, who was here?

Tim Jeremy had come ahead, but Tim would not have come here, in defiance of his instructions, unless Felicity had shown up.

Dawlish pushed the front door wider open.

There was no sound.

He went into the square hall, in which Felicity took such a pride, with its three-hundred-year-old furniture, the Persian carpet, the polished floor. Three doors and a passage led off this. The kitchen door at the end of the passage was shut. The other doors were ajar, as he might have left them.

Except for one thing, everything was normal. The one thing was the silence. The dogs should be barking because he had come, and the cat should be in sight, and Felicity should appear, hurrying, as if—as always—she was delighted to see him, and saying:

"Hallo, darling!"

The cat came stalking in behind him, a big tabby; it went on toward the kitchen.

There was silence.

Dawlish looked into the drawing room on the right. This was really their living room, with the television set and the comfortable chairs, Felicity's work basket, books, a small cupboard with drinks—a comfortable room. It was empty, but there was a distinct smell of tobacco, and he did not think that it was the tobacco of English cigarettes; nor was it Turkish. It smelt rather more like a cigar; and French cigarettes had that kind of smell.

Felicity did not smoke French cigarettes.

Above the door were two crossed medieval daggers, placed there only for decoration. Upstairs in his bedroom, locked away, were two automatic pistols and some ammunition, and outside there were two shotguns and a .22, all used for shooting in the grounds and in the nearby woods. He stretched to the limit of his great height, and took down one of the daggers; it was at least a weapon.

The dining room, with its refectory table and the William and Mary slung leather chairs, was empty.

So was Felicity's morning room.

So was the kitchen.

He looked out of every window, and saw no one.

He turned and went up the stairs, making no attempt to hide the fact that he was in the house. He had a sense of being watched, but knew that might simply be his imagination. The bedroom doors stood ajar; the bathroom door was closed. He opened his own bedroom door, and held his breath, so vivid did a mind picture of Felicity become.

Felicity wasn't there.

Another woman was sitting at her dressing table.

The woman turned around.

She was wearing an off-the-shoulder dress, tied at the neck with a bright red cord. The dress was snow white, with red trimming, and it had a quality which would have made Felicity marvel. This woman also wore a camellia of glorious red in her rich, dark hair, which was a cluster of curls. She was unbelievably beautiful, both of face and of figure. The way she looked around made it seem that she had expected Dawlish, and this was a studied pose.

Her eyes were rounded, and very lovely.

He had never seen her before, but he had seen her photograph often enough, if never quite like this. In this very room, Felicity had shown him a photograph only last night, in the pages of the *Sketch*.

This was Bidot's wife.

There could not possibly be any mistake about it; as the receptionist had implied, you couldn't be in doubt if you saw Marilyn Monroe or Ava Gardner or Mme. Bidot for the first time.

And Mme. Bidot smiled at him, here in his and Felicity's bedroom.

10 CUCKOO

DAWLISH FELT HIS TENSION RISING, felt more wary every second, and watched the woman intently. There was something peculiar about the way she sat there, and for a moment he wondered if she was breathing. She looked more like a dummy than flesh and blood.

She was flesh and blood all right.

In fact, it was an artist's model of a film star's pose; it was almost possible to believe that she expected the camera to click at any moment.

Dawlish did not speak, but went to his wardrobe, bent down and opened the long drawer at the bottom, and unlocked a smaller drawer inside, where he kept his automatics. He opened this.

The guns had been taken away.

Danger had never seemed nearer, but nothing in his expression showed what he felt as he straightened up and turned toward Mme. Bidot.

"Well, well," he said. "Cuckoo."

The woman looked perplexed, but didn't stop smiling. He

went a little nearer to her. She was beautiful—she had everything—and a little more. He thought that she felt as much tension as he did; thought that she was scared.

Of him?

He could understand that, if she was; no doubt he had looked like murder.

But he was completely bewildered, and admitted it. From the beginning, Miller had made a fool of him.

He could be sure of nothing, except that Felicity had been hauled aboard a motorboat and presumably taken toward France, and that Mme. Bidot, wife of a millionaire and the best-dressed woman in Europe, was sitting where Felicity was wont to sit.

A cuckoo in the nest.

What was the matter with him? Was he losing his wits?

She said: "Hallo, Patrick," as if she knew him.

"That's a start," said Dawlish heavily. "You have the name right. Where's my wife?"

"I do not understand you," she said. "Why do you look at me like that?"

Her English was good and her accent attractive; possibly she was exaggerating the accent, like all good actresses could. Her smile was rather brittle, but that did not spoil her loveliness. That milky complexion was almost unbelievable, the coloring superb; only a genius could have known that the red camellia was the one flower in the world which could improve upon perfection.

"Didn't they tell you that my wife's missing, and I have no time for substitutes?" He went nearer, and Mme. Bidot sat absolutely still. Now he felt sure that she was afraid of him or of something. There was quivering tension in her.

"I do not understand, Patrick," she said again.

"You'll understand soon enough," Dawlish said, and drew very close to her. She hadn't moved away, yet he had a feel-

68

ing that she longed to, that the thing she most wanted was to jump up and rush away from him.

Why didn't she?

He stood towering above her and very close, and in order to see his face, she had to tilt her head backward. Her lips were slightly parted; it was easy to know why teeth were so often likened to pearls. A little, faintly blue vein in her throat beat rapidly. With a little imagination, it would be possible to think that he could hear her heart beating. The way she sat, with those parted lips inviting and those deep blue eyes frightened, was a remarkable thing.

He moved his hands.

She sat quite still.

He placed his hands on her shoulders, close to the neck; large, strong hands, with a mat of fair hair on the backs of the fingers. He just rested them there, and did not press.

"I think you understand a lot," he said. "My wife was taken away from Brighton by a friend of yours, one Dr. Maidment. Where is she?"

"It—it cannot be true!"

"It's quite true," said Dawlish, "and I want to know why. I want to know why you're here, too." He squeezed, gently, and now there was no doubt of the fear in her eyes; or that it was of him, and what he would do when he found her here. "Tell me, and tell me quickly, or I'll break your pretty neck in two."

Her breast rose and fell with increasing agitation, but she did not attempt to free herself.

"I had to come here," she said. "I had to see you."

"Who brought you?"

"He——"

"Don't start talking around the houses, just answer my questions and don't waste time," Dawlish said roughly now. "I'm in a mood to strangle the life out of you, and don't forget it. Who brought you here?"

"Claude—Claude Maidment," she declared.

At least, he knew that now. And he had to keep strict control over himself, had to squeeze every possible piece of information that he could.

"When?" he demanded.

"This morning."

"Why?"

She hesitated.

"You know why," Dawlish said, and again his fingers became tight about that slender throat. "And you'll tell me, even if I have to choke it out of you. Why did he bring you here?"

"He—he wishes me to get back the papers which I gave you."

"You didn't give me any papers or anything else," said Dawlish. "Let's have the truth——"

"It is the truth!"

It was a lie, and she knew it; so she was trying to impress someone else. Was that someone here, or was there a microphone or a tape recorder in the room? The questions passed swiftly through his mind as he said with soft emphasis and in a voice which only she could hear:

"And as we've never met before, how and where did you give me these papers?"

"Please, what good will such questions do? I saw you at the Regal Hotel."

He had been to the Regal once or twice lately, to see friends; but he had never seen her.

"You know very well——" he began, but she interrupted.

"That is the truth, and you know it! Now I am to get the papers back from you, that is what Claude requires."

It was fantastic, it seemed crazy, and yet as he scrutinized Bidot's wife and saw the fear in her eyes, it was almost as if she was pleading with him not to call her a liar. He felt the pressure of his fingers in her warm flesh, and realized that he was gripping her more tightly than he had meant to; in

70

those few savage moments, the only thing that had mattered was to make her tell the truth.

He let her go and stood back, but didn't look away from her. She moved her hands to her throat, where his fingers had been, and held them there as if to protect herself; otherwise, she did not move. And she was so beautiful. That was one of the facts that couldn't be evaded. In spite of his fury, in spite of his burning anxiety for Felicity, in spite of everything, he could accept the fact of her beauty, and be stirred by it.

"Listen, Mme. Bidot," he said very gruffly, "there are some things you ought to know. Your husband asked me to meet him in Brighton for lunch today. You were to be with us, and my wife was to come along. I won't go into details, but my wife was kidnapped. Does that mean anything to you? *Kidnapped.*"

"I understand very well," she said.

"And your husband didn't turn up. Instead, he flew back to Paris, after you left the hotel with Dr. Maidment. Why?"

"I was compelled to leave," she said.

"By Dr. Maidment?"

"Yes."

"How?"

"He said that unless I did, Jules would—Jules would be killed."

"Is Jules your husband?"

"Of course."

"And you believed that story?"

"Yes," she said.

"What made you believe it?" Dawlish was looking down at her with narrowed eyes, now, and speaking less roughly. "Why didn't you tell him to go to blazes, and stay at the hotel until your husband came back?"

"I have told you."

"How could Maidment, how could anyone, kill your husband and get away with it?"

She said: "There are some things you do not know, Mr. Dawlish. Three weeks ago, a good friend of my husband was killed. Drowned, you understand. It was a very great shock. He helped my husband in his business—what is it you say? —he was his right-hand man. The drowning was by accident, we thought, and all of us were very sad. Yesterday, Dr. Maidment said that it was murder."

She caught her breath.

She looked as if she had believed just that; and was in fear because of it.

"And if he could kill one, he could kill another," she said. "I believed that my husband was in great danger, and—and I do as I am told."

"Come here, you mean."

"At once, yes."

"With Maidment?"

"With him, and with a chauffeur also."

"Where are they now? Where is their car?"

"I do not know," said Mme. Bidot. "It was perhaps an hour after we arrive that they leave here. They told me that you would soon arrive and that I was to wait for you, in this room. They told me——" she caught her breath again.

"Yes?" asked Dawlish very softly.

She did not go on at once. There was a change in her expression, and it eased the look of fear in her eyes. Her body seemed to relax, too, for the first time since he had come in, as if she realized that the pose was no longer necessary. She closed her eyes; and that was the moment when he saw how long and sweeping her jet black lashes were against the flawlessness of her skin. She raised her hands, as if helplessly, and they no longer protected her throat. When she opened her eyes again, it seemed to Dawlish not only that she was very young and very helpless, but that there was great simplicity about her.

It was easy to believe that she was telling the whole truth; in fact, it was difficult even to remind himself that she might be lying about this as well as about the papers, and might be here simply to fool him, as he had been fooled from the beginning, even into believing that he would see Bidot.

"Go on," Dawlish said at last. "What were you told to do?"

Now, she looked pleadingly at him, and her hands moved toward him, as if she wanted to take his and hold them, and make sure they did not crush her throat.

"They told me that I must get the papers back, even— even if I had to be—be nice to you."

"Nice?" echoed Dawlish almost helplessly.

"They told me that if—if I did whatever you wanted and got them from you, that Jules would not be hurt, either." She continued to stare pleadingly, and then went on in a voice pitched so low that it was difficult to hear. "I will do anything, anything you wish, if you will give me back the papers."

Dawlish said: "So you would." In a moment she would have him believing that he had seen her before, that she had given him these papers. There was no doubt what she meant, as she sat there with those huge shining eyes and that beautiful body, talking like a child, behaving like one, too. It seemed one gigantic hoax, with everything being done to make sure that he couldn't begin to guess what lay behind it.

He remembered all that he had ever heard of her, and some of the things Felicity had told him the previous night. Felicity had a far wider knowledge of such things than he. This girl had been very young when she had gone to Hollywood; only eighteen. She had the body beautiful, and had been a leading model for two years. Some genius had taken her across the Atlantic, and in Hollywood she had been a sensation.

So unworldly, Felicity had said.

Unworldly was the word!

The girl had become the dream of Hollywood because

she was not as other stars were; because she was sweet and simple and so very lovely. A film star made in a convent school. Hollywood had felt both maternal and paternal toward her. Yes, Dawlish could remember these things now, which had been at the back of his mind all day. She had been the photograph pin-up of a million men, she was every man's sister and no man's mistress, no man's to spoil.

Then, she had married Bidot.

That must be how long ago? Five or six years. It had been almost as great a sensation as the marriage of Princess Grace of Monaco. He could remember it now. There had been a lot of gnashing of teeth, talk of baby snatching, sneering articles about the man of nearly forty who could take such a child to wife. It was after all this that she had begun to win her reputation for being the best-dressed woman in Europe.

If she had a face like a hag and a body like a hag, she would still be just a means of finding Felicity.

"Now let's get some things straight," he said. "You didn't give me any papers. We've never met. What's the truth, and where is my wife?"

"I do not know about your wife," she said, and her great eyes seemed to plead again. "Please, give me back the papers. I should never have given them to you."

She had not.

She lied.

It could only be because she believed she was being overheard.

11 NEST

SHE SAT THERE AS IF PLEADING and still touched his hands. She gave no sign that she believed anyone else was within earshot, but she couldn't hope to fool him, so must be putting on this act to fool someone else.

Dawlish freed himself, and she drew her hands back and held them just in front of her breast. The crimson red of her nail varnish matched the crimson of the ribbon which drew the neck of her dress together. He saw that it was tied in a bow. He found himself thinking that with one quick tug, that cord would become undone, and her dress would fall.

She was casting a kind of spell over him.

He moved away, refusing to allow himself to hurry, and watched her all the time. Those were the trusting and pleading eyes of a child.

"Believe me," they said silently. "Please believe me."

He moved toward the wardrobe, looked on top and inside, and then everywhere in the room where there might be a tape recorder or a dictaphone. He found nothing, and he even looked under the mattresses of the twin beds. Bidot's wife watched with those big, beautiful eyes.

He went silently to the door and opened it; no one was outside. He went to the window of the room which overlooked the front garden, the drive, the lawns, some flower beds; and in the distance the hilly countryside, which swallowed the narrow road and hid the village from sight. Three cyclists were passing the gate, but there was no other sign of movement.

Dawlish turned around from the window. He was smiling faintly; he couldn't stop himself. It was a kind of game, with this rare creature. She was the dream of most of the women of the world, was headlined day after day in Europe's press, and here she was sitting and saying that she would do "anything" if he would give her back something she had never given him.

"You have a lot to learn about lying," he said very quietly. "But let's try a change of subject. Did you know that my wife had been kidnapped?"

"No. I told you I did not."

"Did you know she had been threatened?"

"No."

"When did you first hear of me?"

"A week ago," said Bidot's wife.

"Exactly how?"

"It was my husband," she said quite simply, and moved on the stool and sat squarely, her hands resting lightly in her lap. They were slender golden brown hands, like her bare legs and slim ankles; there was no part of her which wasn't beautiful. "He said that he had decided that you were the right man to help him."

"Help him about what?"

"I do not know," said Madame Bidot.

It was like talking to a child; rather like discussing metaphysics with someone who wasn't yet quite sure of elementary mathematics. Dawlish found himself lighting a cigarette, and then went across and offered her his case. She took a cigarette and he leaned forward with his lighter. She touched his hand gently as if to steady the flame, drew in the smoke, and then gave him that quick, bright, simple smile.

"Did you know he was worried and needed help?"

"Oh, yes," she said.

"When did you first find out?"

She gave the vaguest of frowns, as if really trying to remember, and then said:

"I think it would be three weeks ago. We had been to the ballet. It is not his favorite, the ballet, but he knows that I enjoy it, and so whenever there is a short season, we go. I do not know why, but he received a message, and was called from the box. When he returned, he was very troubled."

"Did you ask him why?"

Her eyes seemed to grow larger.

"Of course not," she said. "That was not my affair. He has always told me not to worry about his business."

"And not to worry even when he was worried."

"How would it help, if I did not understand?" asked Mme. Bidot simply. "But it is true, from that day he was not

76

quite so cheerful as before. Worried—perhaps, yes. A little anxious sometimes. He would be eager for telephone messages. There was some talk between him and Maurice, but I did not understand much of it. Then all seemed well. Then Jules was desolated, because Maurice was drowned."

"I see," said Dawlish quietly. "Did he ever suspect that Maurice was murdered?"

"I do not know," said Bidot's wife, as if quite frankly. "I only know that soon afterward we came here from Paris. Then I knew that he was seriously troubled, but he told me to behave as always, and there were the newspaper reporters, the photographers, everything was as usual. It did not seem to me that there was any serious anxiety. But yesterday, after we had seen Claude Maidment for dinner the previous night, I asked him if I could help."

"Please believe me," her eyes pleaded.

"Go on," said Dawlish.

"That was when he said suddenly that you were the one person who could help him," declared Mme. Bidot. "He told me he had come to England to see you and ask for your help, but he could not then see you himself. He said he had reason to believe you were trustworthy, and I was to give you the papers. He also said I must tell you that he would soon see you about these. Later, he made the appointment in Brighton, because he had to go there on some other business. So I expected to go with him to see you at Brighton. But this morning he went out, early, and then Claude came, and—I had to go with him."

"This Dr. Claude Maidment," Dawlish said. "Do you know where he lives in London?"

"No, I do not."

"How often had you seen him?"

"Sometimes when we come to London, sometimes when he comes to Paris, once, last year, at Cannes."

"Is he a business friend?"

"I believe so."

"A friend of the Maurice who died?"

"Perhaps of Maurice, but certainly of my husband. To tell you the truth, Maurice did not like him," went on Mme. Bidot. "Once I heard him talking of it with Jules. Jules laughed, and told him that he was quite wrong."

"Have you no idea at all where I might find Maidment?" Dawlish insisted.

"No," answered Bidot's wife, "I do not know. Now I have told you everything, and I cannot help it if you will not give me back those papers. I have tried my best." She stood up and drew near him. "So many questions, and only two are important. Where is Jules? Where is your wife?" She moved toward the dressing table, unexpectedly, and picked up a photograph of Felicity, a colored one which Dawlish insisted should always be there. It was ten years old, it showed Felicity at her most attractive, and the sight of it brought back sharply the pain of her disappearance; Dawlish felt as if he had been disloyal because, for a while, he had forgotten her in the problem itself.

There was a pause.

"She is very nice," said Mme. Bidot. "I think you are very nice, too."

Dawlish had to force himself to form the next question.

"Did Maidment tell you why he wanted these papers?"

"He said that if I gave them to him, it would help Jules. You see," went on the girl, very quietly, "Claude knows that there is only one important thing in my life. My husband."

She did mean it; she was just being herself. No one could *act* like this.

Except—she'd never seen Dawlish nor given him anything at all.

"That's fine," said Dawlish in a more normal voice. "That means it's easy for you to understand why I want my wife back, and I'd give a fortune to be sure that she isn't hurt. Are you positive there is nothing else you can tell me?"

"I can think of nothing."

"These papers apart——"

"But they are everything!" she burst out. "Everything!"

He felt more than ever certain that she was lying only to impress somebody else. And it was useless to labor the point any more. If he could take her to some place where they were not overheard, where no instrument could be hidden, he would try again.

"All right," he said heavily, "if you remember anything else which might help to explain why Jules was worried and wanted my help, tell me. If you can think of any reason, or can think of anyone besides Maidment who might have frightened him, tell me. A friend of Maidment, for instance."

"I do not know any friends of his."

"Did he ever have a woman with him?"

"Oh, well, yes. At Cannes, there was a woman, yes."

"His wife?"

For the first time, there was a gleam of a smile in the girl's eyes, as if she were amused, and could see the funny side of a remark, was not all sweet simplicity.

"I would not think so."

"What was she like?" asked Dawlish, and took a shot in the dark. "Blonde?"

"Oh, yes, she was blonde. She was not . . ." Mme. Bidot frowned again, leaned back against the dressing table, and went on: "I do not know how to describe her. She was attractive, yes, but she was not beautiful. She was a little big —here." She drew a hand close to her bosom, and then close to her lips. "And here. What is your word? Sexy, yes?"

"Yes, I think that's our word," agreed Dawlish heavily, "and I think I know who it was."

He felt quite sure.

But he did not know what the girl's name was, or where she was just then. Dr. Maidment's girl friend at Cannes had last been seen with Felicity in the motorboat, if his guess was right. She might be back in France, might be in Brighton, might still be at sea.

"If I remember anything, I will tell you," Bidot's wife promised. She hesitated, gave a funny little smile and then went on: "You will forgive me, I hope, if I say that I am hungry. It was not possible to have lunch today, there was but a sandwich. *Please* forgive me——"

Dawlish began to chuckle.

Bidot's wife began to laugh.

Dawlish said, after a moment: "I know what you mean, I didn't exactly have a feast myself. Let's go down and raid the larder." He opened the door for her, and she followed him on to the landing. He had already guessed at the beauty of her movement, and it could not have been more vivid. He let her go ahead, down the stairs. She was as light on her feet as a ballet dancer, and her grace was almost hurtful. From the foot of the stairs she looked around at him, as if asking him which way to go. The way her eyes were rounded, the shape of her parted lips, the way she rested a hand on the banisters, all told the same kind of story. She was a natural seductress.

"Haven't you been in the kitchen before?" Dawlish asked.

"No. I was not allowed anywhere but the room where you found me, until they had gone."

Dawlish said dryly: "I see." He moved with her along the passage by the side of the stairs, to the kitchen. He had already been in here once, and it did not occur to him that anything would have changed. The larder was full, Felicity always stocked up well, and he was famished.

Hideous thought: Felicity was missing, Felicity might be dead; and he was hungry enough to gnaw at a bone.

He pushed open the kitchen door.

He stood stock still, and Bidot's wife bumped into him. He heard her exclaim, but took no notice, and it was fully ten seconds before he said in a strangled voice:

"Tim!"

There was Tim Jeremy, lying back in Felicity's kitchen chair, a wooden one with arms. Tim's arms were tied tightly to the chair. His hair was disheveled. His clothes were torn. There were bruises on his cheeks, his chin and one hand. He looked as if he had been in a fight with a dozen men bigger than himself, and had fought until he was exhausted. Now, he looked so still that it would be easy to believe that he was dead.

Bidot's wife saw him, and cried out.

Dawlish said: "Take it easy," and stepped swiftly toward the chair, still frightened in case Tim was dead. But he could see a faint movement at the other's lips and breast; and when he felt Tim's pulse, he could feel it beating steadily, if a little slowly. He raised Tim's right eyelid and was not surprised to see the tiny pinpoint pupil. Tim had been drugged with morphia or something similar; he might be out for hours.

And while Dawlish had been upstairs with Bidot's wife, Tim had been carried in here, tied to that chair and left.

Where were the men who had brought him? Did Bidot's wife know they were at hand? Was that why she lied about the papers?

Dawlish went to the back door. It was closed. The evening sunlight shone on the vegetable garden and on the orchard, and it was possible to see the reddening fruit of the nearer trees. No one moved. Dawlish went across to the kennels, and his lips tightened when he saw the two Alsatians in there, each looking as dead as Tim.

Each was unconscious.

"But not dead," Dawlish said, in a quiet voice. "Not dead."

He turned to look at Bidot's wife.

She was in the doorway of the house, and there was no doubt that she was more scared than ever. Dawlish moved nearer to her. She did not seem able to look away from him. He tried to tell himself that she did know more than she had admitted, but at heart he did not believe it. She knew no more than Dawlish about this—the only proven lie was her claim that she had given him those papers.

Bidot had wanted to ask him for "help," and that had precipitated all this because Maidment *alias* Miller had discovered what Bidot planned, and had acted swiftly and decisively.

He could have killed Tim, but he hadn't.

Dawlish looked down on the woman who barred his way into the kitchen. Just behind her was Tim, who must be carried upstairs, put to bed, kept warm. Useless Tim, who had been sent here to help, and who should have been full of information.

Every move Dawlish made was anticipated.

Dawlish said to the woman: "What's your name?" quite out of the blue.

"My first name? It is Claire," she told him.

"Claire," said Dawlish, in the same steely voice, "who else knew that your husband was going to ask me for help? Who knew about the arrangement to have lunch together in Brighton?"

"Claude Maidment," she said. "Jules told him when he dined with us. He is the only one."

He was enough, too; there could be no lead through him, unless it was possible to find out his true identity. Dawlish felt sure that Trivett was already busy on that: Trivett would miss little.

"All right, Claire," Dawlish said, and locked the door. "You get supper ready, while I take my friend upstairs. I won't be long."

He expected her to say that she was too frightened to stay

down here by herself, but she did not. She watched him as he cut the cords at Tim's wrists and then carried him, with almost negligent ease. As he went up the stairs one at a time, he kept reminding himself that everything Maidment did had a motive. Leaving Claire Bidot here with him was for a purpose, and must fit into Maidment's scheme.

Was Bidot's wife essential to the scheme?

Would it help if Maidment could be fooled? If Bidot's wife could be taken away from here, for instance, to a place which Maidment did not know? Where he, Dawlish, could make her tell the truth?

Even if it would help, could it be done?

He put Tim on the bed in the spare room, heaped two eiderdowns on top of him, unloosened his shoes, waistband and neckband, and left him. Tim had come through much worse than this.

Dawlish hurried down the stairs.

He felt for a moment almost alarmed, in case Claire Bidot was not there. But she was, and he stood and stared at her and at a hissing gas burner, and saw that she was beating an omelette. Her cheeks were a little flushed, and she was wholly intent on her job.

If Maidment was allowed to make the next move, he could keep on dictating the course of action. Why not beat him to it? Why not leave here, taking Claire with him?

12 SWEET SLEEP

CLAIRE BIDOT LOOKED AROUND from the stove. Her eyes were bright; it seemed as if she had forgotten her fears and her Jules in the delights of cooking. She waved a fork at Dawlish, and called:

"In five minutes, we shall have dinner."

"Wonderful," said Dawlish, and turned and hurried back upstairs, now quite sure that he had to carry the battle to Maidment's camp.

Claire Bidot could be the instrument of attack.

He opened the bottom drawer of Felicity's dressing table, and took out a small box. He unlocked this with a key from the middle drawer. Inside were several small bottles and glass phials—of liquids and tablets. There was also a hypodermic syringe, but he didn't take that. He shook two tablets on to the palm of his hand and, putting them into his pocket carefully, relocked the box and put it away.

As he reached the door, Claire called from downstairs: *"Come and get eet!"*

All her years in Hollywood seemed to echo in that sentence.

Dawlish found himself chuckling as he ran downstairs. Claire was back in the kitchen, and there were two heaped-up plates of food; the omelette looked perfect, chipped potatoes were golden brown, bread was cut, the table was laid French fashion, without a small plate and with only a knife, fork and spoon. Coffee was bubbling gently in the percolator on the electric range.

"Is it good?" Claire asked eagerly.

"Best omelette I've tasted since I was last in France."

"So!" She was as delighted as a child, and suddenly plied him with questions: when had he been to France, did he like the country, which part did he like best, did he like French cooking? And as the talk bubbled from her, so she ate with the appetite of the young; and Dawlish was not far behind.

It was Dawlish who went to pour out the coffee; and, his back to her, dropped the two tablets into Claire's cup. Twenty minutes later she yawned, and tapped her mouth with her fingers. Her eyes had a rather misty look, as if she would fall asleep at any moment.

"It is so silly, I am not often tired like this," she said. "But I can hardly keep awake."

"You've had a busy day," Dawlish told her dryly. "Why don't you go in the front room and lie down? Felicity has one of these bodiline chairs or whatever they call them. I'll show you how they work."

Soon, in Felicity's chair, stretched out comfortably, Claire Bidot was fast asleep.

Dawlish went to a door beneath the stairs, and pressed what looked like a small piece of carving in the wood near it. Another part of the paneling opened. There was nothing really mysterious about this, for during the war Dawlish had been engaged on work considered of great importance, and a special air raid shelter had been provided, not only for him but for the secret documents he had worked on.

The air raid shelter was now used only as a storeroom.

Dawlish pressed another button, and a door opened to reveal a second flight of stairs. He went down. The cellar was freshly painted, sweet-smelling, airy, and there were still some oddments of air raid shelter furniture, including a camp bed, chairs, everything needed for a night underground. He put up the camp bed, and covered it with blankets; then he went upstairs for Claire.

He lifted her, and she did not stir.

He carried her to the cellar, her head lolling against his chest. She was light and easy to carry. He put her on the camp bed, and could not prevent himself from standing and staring at her for what seemed a long time.

Too long.

He drew the blankets over her, and left her. She would sleep for at least eight hours; before she came around he would be here again.

He hurried upstairs to Tim Jeremy, who hadn't stirred.

Dawlish went down again.

He went out, by the back door, walked to the car, and

drove it around to the front door. Then he put out all the lights. There was no indication that the house was being watched, but he felt sure that it was. He went in, collected two big cushions, carried them as he had carried Claire, and put them into the back of the car, taking his time. The moonlight was bright enough for anyone within fifty yards or so to have a good idea of what he was doing; they would be sure that he was putting Claire Bidot in the back of the car.

He took the wheel, and started the engine.

He felt almost as if he was being fooled again; as if he was doing all this for the benefit of watching people who were not there.

He switched on the headlamps.

They showed how dark the night was, and they also showed a man who nipped out of the way from a spot half-way down the drive. Dawlish stepped on the accelerator. The car roared. Another man, at the foot of the drive, jumped in the way of the car and Dawlish saw him vividly —eyes wide open, mouth open too, pale suit, trilby hat— and hand with the gun in it.

There were two flashes of yellow flame. A clanging noise told Dawlish a side was holed. He didn't hear another sound, and the man leapt out of the way. Dawlish reached the gateway, and wrenched the wheel left. Just outside were two parked cars, without lights. Another man appeared, face like a gargoyle's, by the side of one of the cars. Dawlish flashed past him. Foot down as hard as it would go, he roared toward a crossroads from which his house had got its name: Four Ways.

The great danger came from cyclists or motorists using this as a short cut.

Dawlish swung the wheel. Tires screeched. The head-lamps shone on trees and shrubs, the brilliant green eyes of a cat, telephone wires, and, crazily, a boy and girl against the hedge, in each other's arms, turning frightened faces toward him. The girl's mouth was open in a scream which Dawlish didn't hear. The car passed within a foot of them, and for the first time Dawlish relaxed.

"You should do what your mother tells you," he said, as if to the girl.

He reached a wide road, heading for Haslemere. It ran straight for a mile or so, and he switched off the lights and eased off the accelerator, coasting along to the next crossroads. By the time he reached the outskirts of Haslemere he felt quite sure that he had not been followed.

He stopped at a spot where he could turn around easily, took out the cushions and put them behind the hedge, and then got back into the car. He was sweating; he hadn't realized how warm it was. He lit a cigarette, because it would not serve his purpose to go back to the house too quickly; he was as nearly sure as a man could be that Claire Bidot wouldn't be found, even if anyone had gone into Four Ways.

He cooled off, finished the cigarette, tossed it aside, and started off again.

When he came to the crossroads, from where Four Ways was visible by day, and lighted windows of the house could be seen by night, he saw two lighted windows.

So when he arrived, there would be quite a reception party.

He did not drive too quickly, although now he was tense and on edge. He had hit back in the only way he could, but there was no way of telling whether it would bring results. Now that it was done, and his mind was relaxed, he could think of no one but Felicity.

There were no cars at the foot of the drive.

He turned into it, to see lights shining all over the house. That seemed odd, in a way; if Maidment or men working for him were waiting to give him a warm reception, wouldn't they prefer to do it in the dark?

Two cars were drawn up at the front of the house. The

front door was closed, but a man stood in the porch. His right hand was in his pocket, and Dawlish felt sure that he held a gun. Dawlish ignored him, swung the wheel so that the nose pointed down the drive again, stopped and got out. As he turned toward the house, the man moved forward from the porch. Now it was easier to get a clear picture of him.

This was the driver of the Italian sports car, in Brighton that morning.

He held a gun.

"Good evening," said Dawlish politely, and walked straight toward him; they would collide if the man didn't move to one side. Dawlish didn't stop, and the man waited until the last moment, then dodged. "Nice night," Dawlish went on, and stepped on to the porch, tried the handle of the front door and wasn't surprised that the door opened. "Can I help you?" he asked, and went inside, leaving the door open.

Standing and waiting for him was another man, not unlike the one on the porch; and the Bikini Blonde.

13 THE ODD BEHAVIOR OF PATRICK DAWLISH

DAWLISH STOPPED IN THE MIDDLE of the hall. The girl and the man were near the foot of the stairs.

Dawlish felt his heart thump wildly, but it soon steadied. He believed that he had succeeded in carrying the attack to them. They didn't know what to expect and didn't like what had happened, and so they were edgy. That probably wasn't healthy, in view of the gun in this man's right hand, but Dawlish wasn't primarily interested in his health.

"Why, hallo," he boomed, and looked at the blonde, with

his head on one side and his eyes unexpectedly bright. "Didn't you find a wolf on the prom?" He moved toward her, smiling, and neither she nor her companion seemed to know what to do; the man raised his gun a little, that was all. "I suppose I ought to feel flattered, it's not often I'm followed quite so far as this for my manly beauty."

The girl wasn't beautiful, like Claire Bidot, but she had everything else. Now, she wore a lemon-colored linen dress, which was caught at the neck in a high peak, leaving the tops of her arms and her shoulders bare. It was meant to catch the male eye, for about the waist it was as tight and flat as a dress could be, but just above she wasn't exactly flat.

Her eyes told him that she was more puzzled than scared. The man said, "Dawlish, where——"

"Ignore him," Dawlish said. "You didn't come all the way from Brighton to have him play gooseberry, did you?" The girl, startled, began to move back, but he didn't give her time. He took her right wrist and drew her to him, inexorably, and then slid his arms around her back, one at the waist and one at her shoulders. He held her so tightly that she could hardly breathe. She was so startled that she didn't even begin to struggle. She could not avoid looking up at him, and there was sheer disbelief in her eyes.

Quite deliberately, Dawlish kissed her full on the lips.

"Beautiful," he said, and still didn't let her go. She was beginning to look pale from the strain, for his hug was as powerful as any bear's. "Where would you like to go? Out into the moonlit fields? I can recommend a nice haystack, not ten minutes' walk away. Or in the garden shed? There's a hammock, I believe. You'll understand that I'm not anxious that we should consummate our passion inside the house, I'm sure."

He smiled down, and kissed her again.

"You must be crazy!" the man cried. "Let her go!"

"Did you hear that?" asked Dawlish, as if shocked. "You've come all this way to find me, and he wants me to let you go. Then he calls *me* crazy."

"*Let her go!*" the man cried, and Dawlish felt something hard jabbed into the small of his back, and had no doubt that it was the gun. He heard footsteps, too, and knew that the other man had come in from the porch.

The girl gasped, but couldn't speak clearly; she must have felt that the life as well as the breath was being crushed out of her. She began to struggle, but the movements were quite ineffectual; she was like a baby, wriggling. Her eyes held a kind of horror, as if at any moment she expected her bones to crack.

The gun ground into Dawlish's ribs.

"*Let her go!*"

"Go ahead and shoot," said Dawlish, without turning around. "I'll let her go if you put a bullet in my corpus, but where would that get you? Perhaps I ought to say, where wouldn't that get you? It wouldn't get you Mme. Bidot, for instance. Whose bright idea was it to send the lady here?"

"*Let Blondie go!*" The pressure of the gun was getting really painful, and would leave a nasty bruise, but Dawlish didn't ease his hold at all, and didn't even turn his head.

"Oh, yes, Blondie. Sonny Jim, I don't know who told you that you were good at this game, but he was wrong. You're only just beginning. I could crush Blondie to death, and it wouldn't take long. Would it, Blondie?" He increased his pressure and the girl gave a cry, muted but quite clear. "You see what I mean?"

"Let her——" the man began.

Then, he, or the other man, or the pair of them together, struck savagely at Dawlish's head. But they made a mistake, they used their fists, and the blows did not affect him at all. He hunched his great shoulders, still hugging the blonde, and the blows rained harmlessly on top of his head, his neck and his shoulders. Then a man kicked him behind the knees, but he was ready for the move, and did not give way.

"Like to hear her ribs crack?" he inquired.

He could hear the men breathing, knew that they were almost desperate now, and he had come to the end of his play. He waited until the last moment: out of the corner of his eyes he saw a swinging arm. He ducked, let the girl go and pushed her away from him and swung around. One man was swinging at him with the butt of his revolver; the other had grabbed a small chair. Dawlish struck out, using his great arms like flails. He caught one man on the side of the head and sent him reeling, struck the other on the shoulder. This was the man with the gun, who tried desperately to turn the weapon on Dawlish, but before he could, Dawlish wrenched it free.

"Pretty little thing," he remarked. "German manufacture, I see." He spread his left hand, and before the man could get out of reach placed it on his chest and toppled him backward.

The girl, gasping for breath, lay in a heap on the floor. The other man had dropped the chair and was crouching against the wall, gun in hand; but Dawlish now covered him.

Dawlish beamed.

"I wonder who would fire first, Sonny Jim. Supposing we count one, two, three, and then try? Good idea! Get set. One——"

He squeezed the trigger, and the bullet struck the other's gun and sent it whirling out of his grasp, while the man himself cringed back. The gun hit the parquet floor, close to a Persian rug. Dawlish moved across, picked it up and pocketed it, and then turned around to face the trio.

The girl was still huddled on the floor, but she had turned her head around, so that she could see him. The men, crouching, watched, as if they were terrified that he would attack them again.

"I suppose the truth is that no one told you I was the original Strong Man," said Dawlish, as if apologetically. "If I were you, I'd lodge a protest. In writing, say, with carbon copies to the Principal of the School for Thugs." He stood with his back to the door, and although he was talking so freely and seemed intent only on this trio, he was listening keenly for any sound from outside. He heard none; but that did not mean that no one else was there.

He said: "I have one question to ask, and I don't mind which of you answers. But if I don't get an answer, I'll break every bone in each body, starting with the little fingers." He smiled, as pleasantly as if he was asking them how to find the road to London; nothing about him betrayed his burning anxiety. "The question: where is my wife?"

He let the question hang in the air.

None of them answered.

He had never seen two men look more scared than these, yet they kept their lips set. The girl closed her eyes, as if she could not bear to look at Dawlish any longer. The grandfather clock behind Dawlish ticked loudly.

"Blondie," Dawlish said softly, "tell them what it's like."

She kept her eyes closed.

"Sonny Jim," said Dawlish to the nearer of the two men, "you may not believe it yet, but I mean to find out where my wife is. You are going to tell me." This was the man who had driven the sports car, and so was presumably the one who had gone off in the motorboat with Felicity. "Did you hear that? You're the man who is going to tell me where my wife is."

Terrified eyes stared at him.

The man was young, in his early twenties. In his sallow-faced way he was quite good-looking; at times he might even be pleasant. His black hair was thin and rumpled. His light gray suit was rucked up about him, he looked as if he had been blown through the air from a cannon, but he didn't speak.

It wasn't reasonable.

He ought to be so frightened that words would spill out of him, but he didn't say a word. He knew, too. He didn't even attempt to deny that. It was as if he knew that denial would be useless, but he kept absolutely silent.

Why?

Only a greater fear than his fear of Dawlish would keep him from talking.

Was that fear of Maidment?

"I don't think you quite understand," Dawlish said, in the soft and menacing voice. "I want my wife. You know where she is. If you don't tell me you are going to be hurt, and I mean badly hurt. I haven't done Blondie any harm yet, just given her a little friendly hug. If I have to get busy on either of you, you'll curse the day you were born. Where is my wife?"

The man didn't answer.

Dawlish felt coldness inside him, felt it spread from his heart to the rest of his body, like something in the blood stream. He knew he could never carry out his threat, but he was quite sure that these men did not know that. They believed that he meant exactly what he said, had sure proof of his mighty strength, yet they kept silent.

So did the girl.

She hadn't moved, except to draw her legs up a little, so that she was less uncomfortable. Her eyes were wide open, as if in terror. Her body must still be aching. She had had the greatest fright, and she knew where Felicity was.

Dawlish smiled at her brightly.

"Would you like another little cuddle, Blondie?" he inquired. "I've no objection at all. I want just one thing, and you've got a tongue like the others here. Supposing you tell me where I can find my wife."

She didn't answer.

"Blondie," said Dawlish, almost in a whisper, "I mean it. Where can I find my wife?"

He went very close to her.

The breathing of both the men was harsh and labored, and the blonde was holding her breath, as if terrified of what would follow if he hugged her again; but she made no attempt to answer. He would have to take that soft and lovely body into his arms and squeeze and squeeze until she told him.

He held out his arms.

"Come on, Blondie," he invited.

"Don't touch her," one of the men gasped. "Don't touch her any more!"

"Prefer me to work on you?" Dawlish asked softly.

Sweat gathered in tiny beads on his forehead. He did not want to touch the girl again, but any sign of weakness would take away what little chance he had. He felt his heart hammering, and savage anger building up inside. They knew where Felicity was, and he would make them tell him. If he took the girl in his arms again, though, the men would be able to beat and belabor him, and they would probably crack his skull.

He spun around.

The man nearest him reared up, although he hadn't yet been touched. Dawlish moved swiftly, and grabbed him; moved as swiftly to the other man. Each seemed hypnotized. He struck each man beneath the chin, swift, savage blows which knocked them out as swiftly as if he had used a hammer. They slumped down, but he stopped them from falling. He glanced at the girl, who was trying to get to her feet; he wasn't sure whether she had the strength. He went into the drawing room and took the old-fashioned handcuffs from the wall, swung back into the hall, and saw the girl on one knee, now, staring at him with that same dread.

The men were still unconscious.

He handcuffed them together, then hauled them up and perched them on an oak settle, side by side, their heads lolling on their chins. It was like a scene out of a music hall sketch. He turned toward Blondie again; she had gotten to her feet and was holding on to the foot of the banisters for support. Her face was colorless, her lips looked gray. He hadn't noticed it before, but the halter of her dress had broken or come unfastened, and so the peak which had been held up beneath her chin had dropped, and there were her flawless golden shoulders and the curving beauty of her bosom; it was as if, in her fear, she relied on that to stop him from doing what he threatened.

"Blondie," Dawlish demanded, "where is my wife?"

She didn't answer.

"I'm going to make you tell me," Dawlish went on. "Your boy friends can't help you now. Don't make any mistake, I'm going to make you tell me where to find my wife."

Blondie said in a croaking voice: "I don't know!"

"You know perfectly well. You helped to take her out of the water and into that boat. You were with her all the time. Where did you take her, and where is she now?"

Blondie just stood holding on to the banisters, looking as if she would lose consciousness and as if she hadn't the strength to support herself. Such fear; and yet she dared not tell him what he wanted to know.

What could frighten her so much?

That was the thing he had to find out, now. He dared not make a false move, and dared not back out once he tried to force her to talk. Every move had to be tested and proved safe.

Why was this girl so terrified?

Was it fear of what the man named Maidment might do, if she were to talk? Had that silenced the others, too? Was it possible that the influence of a man who wasn't here could be so great?

The influence of a man who wasn't here?

Dawlish felt the shock of understanding, swift and savage and, for the moment, almost unnerving him. No one would be so affected by someone who wasn't here, so—Maidment was here. Maidment was watching, he knew everything that was happening, he had managed to imprison them in a fear of himself which was greater than the fear of Dawlish.

Was that it?

Was Maidment at the landing? Was he standing, unseen but seeing everything, perhaps covering them with a gun? Was that what had frightened them?

If he was . . .

Don't let him know that he's been seen, Dawlish told himself, don't look for him, don't be lured into making a mistake. Go on as if there was no possibility of being watched.

"Blondie," Dawlish said again, "I don't want you to make any mistake about it. As soon as your boy friends come around, we are going to get busy, and you won't like it. Here's a chance to tell me without letting them know what you've done. That's what's been holding you back, isn't it? If they know you've talked, they'll tell Maidment."

The girl caught her breath.

"Take it easy and tell me," Dawlish urged, standing very close, so that he could take her in his arms with a single movement. "I don't want to make you suffer, but——"

He heard a sound, just a little tinkle, as of something fragile breaking, and then he saw something glint as it flew past his face. Next moment, there was a small wisp of vapor, and he felt a sharpness biting at his nose and his mouth. He backed away, darting a glance upward. He saw nothing except the vapor, spreading everywhere now, making him cough and choke, making him helpless.

He couldn't do a thing.

14 GIANT IN CHAINS

DAWLISH DID NOT lose consciousness.

He was aware of the pain at his eyes and nose and mouth, and of the fact that although he beat at the vapor and backed away, there was nothing he could do to stop it from enveloping him. He came up against the wall, crouched against it, felt the tears rolling down his cheeks, knew that this was tear gas, so concentrated that it made him helpless. Then, hands gripped him. He felt himself being half pushed and half dragged away from the wall. He thought that he was being taken into the drawing room, but couldn't be sure. He could hardly breathe, and there was agony at his nose and eyes, his mouth seemed to be on fire. Then he was pushed into a chair; he had not the sense, then, to know that it was the carver's chair in the dining room, with its stout wooden back and stout wooden arms. He heard a clanging noise, but didn't recognize it; and then he felt himself being yanked back against the chair, felt cold steel at his wrists.

He was being chained to a chair.

The dog's lead chains were being used.

He felt something else being tied around his ankles, to the legs of the chair. He knew that he couldn't move, and he couldn't even put his hands to his face, in order to try to ease the pain.

Then, the hands left him. He sat alone for what seemed a long time, but it was not really long. Someone actually bathed his eyes and face; then dried them; then put a cup to his lips. Cool liquid soothed his mouth. He was not himself again, but felt infinitely better than he had; then the soothing bathing and the soothing drink was given again, and he felt almost comfortable.

There was a light in front of his eyes, but he could not see properly, tears still welled up.

The light went out.

There was darkness and silence, and he sat helpless, chained to that chair. The chains had been bought to secure dogs so powerful that there must be no risk of letting them escape; and the dogs were doped and their chains were around him. He had no chance to get away.

So he had to sit here, in the silent darkness.

And he had not found Felicity, and had done nothing to help her.

He knew that he had been in this chair for over an hour, and that it was past midnight. Twice the silence had been broken by the striking of the grandfather clock, just by the door. Eleven . . . twelve. The day was over, a new one begun. And the silence and the darkness were still all about him.

Then, out of it, came a voice.

"Dawlish," a man said.

Dawlish jerked his head up, but didn't respond.

"Dawlish."

After a pause, Dawlish said huskily, "What is it?"

"You can't get away. You are as helpless as your wife. Do you realize that?"

The voice sounded like that of an Englishman. It came from the window, and he could imagine the man sitting on the window seat—in Felicity's favorite position. She would sit there with her legs drawn up, working at her tapestry, pausing now and again to glance out of the window into the garden; little things, like the antics of birds or the humming of the bees or the sight of a sparrow or a thrush having a bath, always entranced her.

"Dawlish, answer me."

Dawlish said: "Where is my wife?"

"You are quite as helpless as she is," the speaker said. "I'm very interested to hear that you're so much in love with her. She really matters to you, doesn't she?"

Dawlish didn't answer.

"You shouldn't have made that so clear," the speaker said mildly. "I grant that I had a good idea of that, before I arranged to take her away. The best place to attack a man is in his weakest spot."

Dawlish didn't respond.

The speaker said: "Don't be sullen, Dawlish, or you'll get more punishment than you expect. Something like this, for instance."

Nothing happened.

There was the silence; the darkness; a sudden realization that the blinds and the curtains were drawn, to hide the moonlight, but that was all. The speaker had said "something like this" and had left it in the air, but still nothing happened. Was that deliberate? Was this part of the war on Dawlish's nerves? If it was, it was successful. He gritted his teeth against whatever might come, and the longer he waited with nothing happening, the worse the menace seemed to be. From the beginning, it had been as if these people had meant to make a fool of him and they were doing it, they——

A shock ran through his body.

He cried out.

He felt it burning his arms and his back and his legs, a vibrating series of shock waves one after the other. After the first moment he knew exactly what it was, and clenched his teeth to make sure that he didn't cry out again, but it was not easy; now and again he felt as if he would have to scream.

The torture stopped.

His whole body was a mass of quivering nerves.

"People get electrocuted that way," the speaker announced casually. "It is only a matter of how many volts

99

pass through the body. We simply attached a live wire to those chains of yours—simple, isn't it?"

Dawlish was sweating, and clenching his teeth now against another shock. The fact that he knew what it was didn't really make it any easier; the bad thing was it might come out of the silence, without any warning at all.

This man was truly expert.

"Dawlish," the speaker said, in his nonchalant voice, "you can rejoin your wife, and forget that this ever happened, if you'll be sensible. There's no need for more of this, provided you've come to your senses. Just answer two questions. Where did you take Mme. Bidot?" There was a pause, not lengthy, but just long enough to allow the question to sink in. Then, as casually as ever, came the second question: "And where are the papers?"

Dawlish felt half stupid; and that was how the speaker meant him to feel. He might talk; but he could never talk about papers of which he'd never heard until an hour or so ago.

"Just give me the two answers, and we can stop all this," the speaker went on. "But if you refuse to tell me . . ." There was a slight chuckle in the quiet voice, but it didn't make Dawlish feel at all light-hearted. "If you refuse to answer, I'll know the truth about your devotion to your wife. What comes first, Dawlish, your charming wife or a fortune?"

Papers?

Fortune?

"Where is Mme. Bidot?" the speaker demanded.

It wouldn't be long before that current was switched on again. Any moment, now. Dawlish stiffened himself, trying to get ready for it when it came, but that wouldn't help, he might steel himself against crying out, but that was all. He didn't know how long he would be able to stand out against this.

He flinched.

100

There was a sharp attack of the current, and he held his breath.

It died away.

"Dawlish, I mean what I say," the man said. "I mean it just as much as you did when you were talking to Blondie and the others. I was up on the landing, listening. Answer me just two questions: where is Mme. Bidot, and where are the papers?"

He would switch that current on again . . . .

Dawlish made himself say: "Oh, Claire is staying with friends." He meant it to sound flippant, but his voice was too hoarse and unsteady for the full effect, and he had a sudden fear that it would only make the other angry and more vicious. "I'll make a bargain," he went on, "Bidot's wife in return for my wife."

"You haven't got a ghost of a chance," the speaker said in a voice which was undoubtedly less nonchalant; he seemed a little nearer, too, and Dawlish believed that he had gotten off the window seat, and was stepping toward him. "I don't want there to be the slightest misunderstanding. I want Mme. Bidot back, and I want those papers. From then on, you will be no more important to me than a London policeman."

Silence.

There was a sound of movement, almost furtive, and it seemed quite near. There was the fear that the current would be switched on again, too. Dawlish tried to steel himself against the pain, tried to wonder what would happen when he kept silent.

The current.

It came.

He would not be able to last out. Even though the current was off again, his nerves were twitching, sweat dripped down from his forehead, and his mouth was quivering. This was something different from anything he had known before. He believed that he would talk, that he would tell the speaker where to find Bidot's wife, but——

He couldn't tell him anything about the papers; he knew nothing about them.

Would the other believe him?

"Dawlish, I am going to convince you that I mean exactly what I'm saying," said the man in the darkness. He was closer, and Dawlish believed that if he could stretch out a hand, he could touch the other. "Just two things, and you'll be released and your wife will be unhurt. It's very simple. Where is Mme. Bidot, and where are the papers which Bidot sent to you?"

The papers which Bidot sent.

The house that Jack built.

Papers.

"I don't know what you're talking about," Dawlish said, and was glad that his voice sounded more normal, and was not so edgy and rough. "No one gave me any papers. I have never met Bidot. He telephoned me last night and asked me to meet him in Brighton today. That's as near to Bidot as I've ever been."

Did it sound convincing? At least it came out flatly, factually.

There was a longer pause than before, until the speaker said:

"It's no use lying, Dawlish. I want to know where the papers are."

"Until Mme. Bidot said her piece, I'd never heard of these papers."

"Dawlish," said the man in the darkness, "you don't seem to understand the position at all. You are quite helpless, and so is your wife. You have to decide between seeing her again or knowing she will die. You have to make up your mind quickly, too. I mean to know, and I'm not going to leave

102

here until I do. Where is Mme. Bidot, and where are the papers?"

Only the darkness was between them now, and the man's soft breathing. Then there came a different sound—as of a man outside, hurrying. In the distance there were noises, too, of car engines. Cars by the dozen passed the end of the drive, and in the night following August Bank Holiday late drivers weren't exactly freaks. Those outside sounds seemed divorced from the quiet of the room, and from the awful choice which faced Dawlish.

He said: "Mme. Bidot's somewhere quite safe from you. She didn't give me any papers. Nothing I can say can help you. Nothing you do or can say will lead to Bidot's wife."

He heard the other man draw in a sharp breath and then went on, "So don't waste——"

"Blondie!" The man's voice cut across Dawlish's words, and he realized that the girl had been there, although he hadn't heard her. "Blondie, go and tell Paul to stop——"

He broke off; and obviously he was no longer thinking about Dawlish.

Footsteps sounded in the hall. Now Dawlish took notice of them, for a man was running. There were the sounds of car engines not far away, then the noise of gears being changed. All drivers had to change down when they were swinging around for this steep drive.

Who . . .

The door burst open, and light from the hall streamed through. It shone on the girl, who was nearer the door, and on a tall, thin-faced man standing closer to Dawlish, facing the door now, so that all Dawlish could see was his sharp profile, the hooked nose, the pointed chin.

"I told you not to come in here unless——"

"Two police cars are on the road!" a man gasped. He had been running so fast that he could hardly get the words out. "They're coming here, one of them's halfway up the drive now. Paul's blocking the drive. We—we haven't much time."

He broke off.

The sound of a roaring engine came much more loudly through the open doors; and then a car horn blared out insistently.

The thin-faced man with the striking profile swung around on Dawlish, slapped him on the side of the face, and leapt toward the door. The girl was already outside; the other man darted in the tall man's wake.

The horn was still blaring.

15 THE POLICE

DAWLISH SAT UP IN THE CHAIR, head erect, face toward the open door. The confusion outside seemed greater, and he had heard the last three shots. Men were running up or down the drive, but seemed to get no nearer. Doors slammed. A car engine started up. There was a cart track which ran alongside the grounds, an emergency exit which Dawlish had used once when the drive was blocked, and Maidment's men might know about that.

Footsteps drew nearer.

Someone called: "Be careful!"

"The hell with that, I'm going in."

"Be *careful*."

There was a moment's pause, then a scurry of footsteps. Dawlish saw a shadow, and guessed that one of the police had run in from the porch, and was now crouching against the wall. A man from outside called:

"All clear?"

"Seems like it."

"Okay."

As still more men came hurrying up the drive, a policeman in uniform appeared in the doorway. He did not see Dawlish at first, because the door hid him from view; so Dawlish said, "This way," and realized his voice was little more than a croak. But it worked, for the man pushed the door back and strode in—saw Dawlish in the dim light, paused, and flashed a torch into Dawlish's face.

"Good God!" he exclaimed. "Let's have some light on the scene."

"*No,*" cried Dawlish. "Don't touch that light!"

"Why on earth——"

"Sorry." Dawlish was sweating more now than he had all the time of the ordeal. "The cable comes from a plug. Okay, switch on." He gulped. The words seemed to hurt the back of his throat. He stared at the policeman, who could now make out an electric cable leading from a wall plug to the man in the chair. He turned around and switched on the light, and for the first time saw exactly what was in the room: a giant chained to a carved oak chair, sweating face a pasty gray. "Take that damned plug out, will you?" Dawlish begged. "I won't feel safe until then."

The man obeyed.

Another man, in plain clothes, came in, saw Dawlish, and stood gaping.

The uniformed man said: "Looks as though they tried to electrocute him, sir."

Dawlish found himself giving a set grin, and kept it up while the two men worked and the chains were loosened and he was free. He felt absurdly like fainting, but didn't. He took a sip of whisky from a proffered flask, and soon felt almost able to think and to feel again.

When he stood up, his legs were wobbly, but he reached the hall without any help. The sliding door which led to the air raid shelter was closed; he should have known that it would be, that there had been no time for the others to reach it, and find the secret of opening it. Claire Bidot was in that sweet, drugged sleep down below, and none of these police realized it. So far, they had looked but not asked their questions, and Dawlish knew why. These were not senior men, but soon a Superintendent or at least a Chief Inspector would be on the way.

"Sure you're all right, sir?" a man asked.

"I'm improving," Dawlish said. "I wish—hallo, do I hear a car?"

"It will be Superintendent Trivett, I expect, sir."

"Bill Trivett?" Of course it would be. "Of the Yard?" Silly question.

"That's right, sir. He happened to be at Haslemere when the report came through that there was some trouble here. He's on his way."

"Well, that could have been a lot worse," Dawlish said. "Have you searched upstairs?"

"Yes, sir. There's a man unconscious on a bed—looks as if he's been drugged."

Tim.

"He has," said Dawlish. He watched the lights of a car which was coming up the drive, now cleared of obstructing cars, then went into the kitchen, rinsed his mouth and bathed his eyes again, then had a long, cool drink. He heard brisk footsteps, and turned to see Trivett and a local Chief Inspector come bustling into the room. Trivett was just Bill Trivett, alert and bright-looking, almost a little too handsome to be true. The local man was bulky in brown; and his name was Brown. He and Dawlish were acquaintances.

"Now what?" Trivett demanded, and his attitude said that he meant to have all the answers.

"Trouble, Bill," said Dawlish, almost inanely. "Really bad men, too. How did you hear that something was on?"

"Never mind that. What——"

"Don't be difficult," Dawlish pleaded. "I've had a night to remember, and I ought to be fried. I mean, electrocuted," he added very carefully. "I've never known a neater way of opening a man's mouth. How did you work your miracle?"

"I'd sent word to have the Surrey Police keep an eye on this place," Trivett said, seeing that he would get nowhere until he replied. "They weren't able to come right away, nearly everyone was out on traffic duty, there was a twenty-mile crawl at Hindhead. So they arrived late. A cyclist had been knocked off his machine and badly injured, just outside your gate, and everyone concerned thought it was an accident. Then a doctor identified a bullet wound. As soon as we heard, we were on our way. I'd come down to Guildford anyhow, had to pick Grace up—she was with her parents. Now," Trivett went on brusquely, "what happened here?"

Dawlish began to explain.

But he hadn't yet made up his mind how much to tell.

He could safely tell Trivett about the papers, which Bidot was supposed to have given him, and he did. Trivett seemed to be as mystified as he was himself. He could tell him exactly what had happened when the attack had been made and could even explain what he had done to Blondie. He could tell him to go after Dr. Claude Maidment, too.

Should he tell Trivett that Bidot's wife was in the air raid shelter?

She was important to the man who had questioned him; she was a hostage, now, and he might be able to play her off against Felicity. But if he told Trivett, Trivett would have to see her and might insist that she should be taken away from Four Ways. If he had an ace up his sleeve, Dawlish decided, the ace was Claire Bidot. If he didn't tell Trivett and the police discovered afterward he would probably have to pay for it, but the future was unimportant. He needed an ace to play as he had needed nothing else in his life.

So he didn't tell Trivett about Claire Bidot.

At half past one the police discovered three microphones and a recording set, all very small; the bedroom, kitchen and living room were connected to it, and he felt sure that Mme. Bidot had known and therefore persisted in her lie about the papers. It was as well Dawlish had told Trivett so much, for now everything he and the Frenchwoman had said could be transcribed.

It was two o'clock before the police left Four Ways. By then every inch of every room had been examined for clues, and Dawlish wasn't sure whether the police had discovered anything that would help. Men had searched the grounds, too. One car had been parked at the side of the house, and the girl and the three men had escaped in that, using the cart track and taking a shortcut to the road. There was some talk of tire tracks, and various police calls were out but Dawlish was in the dark about most of what the police had done. A second car—the one used to block the drive—had been examined for prints, and a description of it was being flashed to London and the surrounding counties. It carried false number plates, and Dawlish doubted whether the police were hopeful.

He wasn't hopeful at all.

Two policemen were on duty in the front garden and two at the back; Trivett was quite prepared for further trouble. He did not intend that Dawlish should face it on his own. There was little doubt that Trivett, who knew him well, suspected that Dawlish had kept vital information back. He, Dawlish, would be closely watched, but that didn't greatly worry him.

The problem of his own next move did.

Blondie and the others weren't likely to come here, while the police were watching. Yet he had to contact them again. He had no idea where they might be, but suspected that they would be watching him, if only from a distance. Sooner or later they would have to make another attempt on him. He mustn't let it happen until he felt thoroughly capable of coping. It would be crazy to take a risk by acting when he was only at half pressure.

Felicity hovered in the background of his mind; like a ghost.

But he had to have a few hours' rest, and had to talk to Claire Bidot again.

There was a problem; what to do with Claire when she came around. The Four Ways' servants, who had been away for the holiday weekend, would be back in the morning; the air raid shelter wouldn't really be safe when they were around. They certainly couldn't be trusted not to tell the police if he asked them to take food down to Claire.

He had a lot of thinking to do, and half of the problems seemed insoluble.

A few hours' sleep might help him.

He could hardly keep his eyes open.

It was nearly a quarter to three when he opened the door in the staircase wall, and went down, very quietly, as if there was a risk that he would wake Claire. As he reached the foot of the stairs, he had a wild idea that she wouldn't be there; but she was. He went nearer. She was lying in exactly the position she had been when he had left her, so still and pale that there seemed to be a risk that she was dead.

Crazy!

Her pulse was beating, she was breathing, she would come out of the drugged sleep in four or five hours.

That was how much time he had.

He dragged himself upstairs to bed, to the bedroom which last night and so many nights before he had shared with Felicity. He made himself look at Tim, who hadn't moved either. Tim might be all right in the morning, though. Tim and Ted—Ted would be in Paris by now, with luck he would have had some results, too.

Unless he had also run into trouble——

Dawlish pulled off his shoes, loosened his belt and dropped on to the bed.

"Must wake at seven," he told himself. "Must wake at seven."

He would have put on the alarm, but was too tired.

He went to sleep.

He felt his shoulder being shaken, and heard his name being called, and was vaguely aware that it was a man's voice, and not Felicity's. He didn't remember what had happened at first, just wanted to be left alone. His head was so heavy that he couldn't get it off the pillow, and his eyes would not open. The shaking continued, and so did the shouting, and he felt angry with whomever it was, and tried to wave him away. But he couldn't. Then he recognized his name, and realized that Tim Jeremy was shouting at him.

"Wake up, Pat.

"Wake up!

"Pat, there isn't any time to lose, wake up!

"*Wake up!*

"Wake——"

There might be news of Felicity!

On the instant when he remembered what had happened and realized what this might mean, Dawlish was wide awake. He pushed the bedclothes ba̶c̶k̶ a̶n̶d̶ forced his eyes open. The back of his head seemed to be falling off as he stared up at Tim. Tim didn't look any the worse for his ordeal, except for the bruises, and they had been patched up. Tim would take punishment with any boxer.

"Felicity?" Dawlish croaked.

"No. Ted's on the wire."

"Eh? Ted?"

"On the telephone. From Paris."

"Ted is—oh. *Ted!*" Dawlish grabbed the receiver of the telephone, which was next to the bed, and shouted into it: "Hallo, Ted! You all right?"

110

Ted Beresford's voice was so plain and deep that he might have been in the next room. Dawlish felt his own heart steadying, and saw Tim backing away from him and standing and staring down. There was a bedside clock, and it must have stopped last night, for the hands pointed to eleven o'clock. It couldn't be so late.

"I'm fine," Ted said. That was one relief, he and Joan hadn't run into trouble. "I've called to find out if you want me to tackle Bidot myself."

"What?"

"Shall I tackle Bidot and see if he can tell us anything, or will you?"

"You mean you've found Bidot?"

"That's what you sent me over for, isn't it? He's at his Paris apartment, near the Bois de Boulogne. Joan and I are having a *citron pressé* at a café opposite. What are the orders, Pat?"

Dawlish hesitated. Tim scratched his chin. Funnily enough Tim, who shouldn't have come around until eight o'clock at least, and it couldn't be more than eight now, was freshly shaven.

"Don't stay asleep *all* day," Ted Beresford protested.

"Sorry," said Dawlish. "Ted, I'm coming over on the first available plane. Don't lose Bidot. Be careful, though, you could run into a lot of trouble. If I can't get a BEA flight pronto, I'll come over in a biplane. The vital thing is to hold Bidot where he is, he mustn't get away."

"Leave it to me," said Ted, and sounded positively cheerful. "Over my dead body. How are you, old boy? From the sound of you, you've been having nightmares."

"Call it that," agreed Dawlish. "Fine, Ted. 'Bye."

He rang off.

"In view of the obvious possibility that you would want to go to Paris, *maestro*," said Tim Jeremy sardonically, "I have arranged with the Surrey Flying School to have a biplane at your disposal, fueled and ready. The airfield is twenty minutes' drive away. The plane is a two-seater, and I'm coming."

He gave a charming smile, and his face looked thinner than ever.

"No," said Dawlish. "I——"

"Yes."

"Tim," said Dawlish earnestly, "I'll have a cup of tea, and then we'll get some breakfast and I'll explain. There's a job you can do here."

"Lunch," insisted Tim firmly. "It is now almost twelve noon, but a man with eyes as bloodshot as yours at the moment can hardly be expected to tell the time. Your so-called treasure is downstairs, telling herself that well-she-nevered. Old Dan is in the orchard, and he's fed the pigs. The two dogs are a bit down in the mouth, but otherwise all is normal. The house can look after itself. I'm coming with you."

Dawlish got out of bed.

"Tim," he said, "go and get Bessie to make a cup of tea, my mouth is like sandpaper. Then send her down to the village—give her a note for the doctor, that'll do. She jumps at any chance of leaving the house. Ask Dan to go to the far end of the orchard and have a look at those Bramleys which are rotting—if we've brown rot that means trouble. And then I want to show you something."

"I am coming to Paris," asserted Tim.

Bessie the daily help was on her way to the village. Old Dan was on his slow and painstaking way to the far end of the orchard. Dawlish opened the door beneath the stairs, and Tim held the coffee and toast on a tray. He did not seem convinced that Dawlish was serious. Dawlish listened intently as he went downstairs but heard nothing. He had the same sense of alarm that he had known the previous night, and it was just as pointless.

There was Claire Bidot.

She was sitting in a garden chair, looking idly through

112

some old fashion magazines. No one would ever know how she managed it, but she looked fresh and so beautiful that she wasn't quite real. She started up when Dawlish called her name, but her nerve was remarkably good, because it was only a start. She wasn't frightened now.

"Tim," said Dawlish mildly, "this is Mme. Bidot, known as Claire to her friends. Someone has to stay and look after her, or she might run into trouble. Will you stay?"

Claire looked from one to the other, wondering what this was all about.

"Okay," Tim said, at last. "I'm on."

Now Dawlish had to persuade Claire that the wise thing to do was to stay here.

She agreed, for she had little choice.

But she admitted that she knew everything would be overheard, so she had stuck to her lie about the papers.

"If I had not, Maidment would still think Jules had them," she said simply. "And he would then torture Jules."

"Better me than Jules, of course," Dawlish said heavily.

"But of course," Claire Bidot said quietly.

16 FLIGHT TO PARIS

THERE WAS A STRANGE LOOK ABOUT TIM when he and Dawlish reached the hall, and the door slid to behind them. He didn't speak at first, but led the way into the front room, and went straight to the cocktail cabinet; for many years he had regarded Four Ways as his second home. He smiled wryly as he asked:

"Care for a drink?"

"I never drink before breakfast," said Dawlish.

"Ah," said Tim, and poured whiskey and soda. He held it

up against the light, examining it critically, and then he sipped and asked abruptly: "What's the matter with her? Is she as simple as she seems?"

"Simple?" Dawlish echoed. "Is that the word?"

"It's damned near it. A dumb brunette, if you prefer it that way. It's like talking to a child, not a grown woman."

"And you think it could be an act?"

"Don't you?"

"I've given her the benefit of the doubt," Dawlish said, "but you might be able to change my mind. I'm telling Bessie that we're going away for a few days, and she needn't come in," Dawlish went on. "Old Dan will be in and out of the garden but he won't come near the front of the house unless you send for him. That leaves you in sole charge. Neither the police nor bad men nor strangers ought to know that Claire Bidot is here. I've an idea that the house will be watched," added Dawlish, "and Maidment and his boy and girl friends may still think that I took Claire off to the village. I'd better lay something on which makes it look as if I've taken her away." He rubbed his chin, while staring at Tim, and went on: "What I need is a pretty little brunette who might look like Claire Bidot from a distance. Any ideas?"

"You are a louse. My kid sister."

"Think she'd like a few days in Paris? Entirely on her own and away from danger once we've taken her off?"

"I think it possible that she could be persuaded," Tim said dryly. "Shall I call her?"

"Will you? Ask her to come to the pub in Alum, to a room I'll arrange to reserve. Then I'll collect her, and we'll nip off to the airfield."

"While I remain bodyguard here?"

"Yes."

"You might need a bodyguard yourself," Tim reminded him.

114

"The police will look after me," declared Dawlish solemnly.

For there were policemen at the gate and policemen in the grounds. It was not surprising that Trivett had not taken everything Dawlish had said at its face value. Trivett would be anxious to find out exactly what was happening yet be willing within reason to allow Dawlish his head. There were times when Dawlish believed that it was wise to consult the police on his next step, and this was one of them.

After Tim had telephoned his sister, Dorothy, and reported that she couldn't get to Alum fast enough, Dawlish first arranged for a room at the village inn and then telephoned Scotland Yard. It was half past twelve, and Trivett was in his office. He sounded non-committal, when Dawlish said:

"I thought I'd better tell you what I'm up to, Bill. . . . Bidot is at his apartment in Paris, and he ought to know what these papers are about. I'm flying over to see him."

"Any news of Felicity?"

"No."

"Pat," Trivett said slowly, "you know the stakes you're playing for, don't you?"

"I know them," Dawlish said quietly. "No one ever won high stakes or low by appeasing the other side. Bill . . ."

"Yes?"

"Any reported accidents at sea? Drownings, or suchlike?"

"I've checked every report from the south coast, and there's nothing," Trivett assured him.

"Thanks."

"And I'll keep checking," promised Trivett. "You might like to know that we haven't found a trace of the people who were at Four Ways last night, but we picked up several fingerprints. And in case you think that we're sleeping, I've been talking to the *Sûreté Nationale* in Paris. Except that his partner and general manager, a man named Maurice Dillon, was drowned in an accident a few weeks ago, there's nothing they can tell us about Bidot. He has an extremely good reputation, and the police don't know of any trouble."

"Meaning exactly?" asked Dawlish mildly.

"You might get away with things over here because I and a lot of other thick-headed idiots let you," Trivett said. "That won't apply in France. Don't run into trouble with the police over there. You won't find a Paris jail as comfortable as one of ours. And be careful how you deal with Bidot. Don't try to stand him on his head and shake information out of him."

"Now, Bill," said Dawlish softly, "you've forgotten something. I'm looking for Felicity."

All the rest was unimportant. He could act as if there was nothing to worry about. He could behave like a clown, could sound light-hearted. But beneath all these things there was iron in his soul, because Felicity was missing and he did not know where to find her.

He only knew that he could not sit back and wait for Maidment to attack; he had to be on the move.

The Anro two-seater biplane began to lose height, about twenty miles from a Paris which was clearly visible as a great dark mass against the green of the countryside. Dawlish, sitting next to Dorothy Jeremy, who was gaping raptly out of the plane's small window, liked the gleam in her eye and the way she had behaved. It wasn't really surprising in Tim's sister, of course. She had driven from London in an old sports car at a speed which had made him, Dawlish, open his eyes. When he had arrived at the inn, she had been waiting, agog with excitement, in a bedroom at the back. She'd played her part eagerly. And to help fool any of Maidment's men who might be watching, Dawlish had taken Claire Bidot's hat and gloves, which were likely to be recognized. He had hustled Dorothy into his car and driven at speed to the airfield near Guildford. The police had followed, but as far as he had been able to find out, no one else had taken any particular interest.

Dawlish was more on edge than he had expected to be.

He couldn't understand why Maidment hadn't tried to get in touch with him. A letter, a telegram, a telephone call, even a messenger, would not have surprised him, but the silence did. It was almost a repetition of what had happened yesterday; Dawlish was being pushed around because he did not know what the next move against him would be.

He couldn't be sure that it would help when he saw Bidot.

"Are we going down now?" Dorothy asked, and turned to look at him with clear, gray eyes. She wasn't a beauty, but her complexion hadn't a flaw, and few men would fail to notice her figure.

"Should land in ten minutes," Dawlish said.

"Oh, what a pity!"

"Enjoyed it?"

"It's been wonderful!" Dorothy put a hand on his arm, and looked intently into his eyes; he wondered what was coming, sure only that she was going to ask some favor or other. "Pat, darling."

He kept a straight face.

"Yes, Dot, dear."

"Is there anything I can *do* for you in Paris?"

"There certainly is," said Dawlish, and he took both of her hands in his, while the pilot in the cockpit put the nose of the plane downward against the wind. "You can go to the Lido, the Folies and the Opera, and tell me if the quality has been maintained. And you can eat at——"

"Pat, I'm serious."

"I am serious, too," said Dawlish quietly, and squeezed her hand. "Listen, Dot. Felicity's in a really bad jam, and you know it. First and last, I want to find her. I don't want to need to worry about you. I don't want to find myself distracted by having to look for you, if these people should decide that you're worth taking away. They could. You're coming with me in a taxi which I've laid on. I'm going to shake off anyone who might follow us, and drop you at a Metro. Then you'll go to the hotel that Tim told you about. Stay as long as you like, but make sure you don't get yourself mixed up with anyone named Dawlish. That's absolutely vital."

She was obviously disappointed, but said, "All right, Pat."

"Don't let me down," Dawlish said, very softly.

Five minutes later, they were on the ground. Ten minutes after that, they were through customs. A large Citroën with a good turn of speed was waiting for Dawlish, who took the wheel, which was on the "wrong" side of the car to him, as if he had been driving with the wheel on that side all his life. He watched the driving mirror closely; three cars started off more or less at the same time. One roared ahead toward the city and the others dropped a long way behind. Dawlish felt quite sure that they hadn't been followed. Soon, they reached the tall, narrow houses on either side of the wide road, passed the small shops with their attractive windows, the *patisseries*, the *boucheries*, the shops with their windows filled with long, crusty rolls, the children walking, the men cycling, the women hurrying, with long loaves tucked under their arms or tied to bicycles. All of these things Dorothy stared at as if she hadn't seen them before, although she knew Paris well. Traffic grew thicker. *Gendarmes* blew their whistles gustily, and waved their white batons urgently, and the traffic surged forward in one rush, or else stopped as if a hundred brakes had been jammed on at the same moment. There was a strange silence, for Paris horns no longer sounded with strident anger.

Dawlish still felt sure that he hadn't been followed.

He saw a Metro station a few hundred yards along, slowed down, and stopped; and Dorothy slid out of the car and slammed the door, blew him a kiss, and hurried toward the subway as if she knew that he did not want to waste a second. He smiled as he watched her going, walking briskly and gaily and with legs nearly as neat and shapely as Claire Bidot's.

And Felicity's.

It was only a ten-minute drive to the Bois de Boulogne, and it took hardly any time to find Bidot's apartment block. From the first glance, luxury was obviously the key word, for outside the main entrance huge Cadillacs, Chryslers and Rolls-Royces were parked, and at the wheels of many of these were patient chauffeurs. One of these chauffeurs, wearing a peaked hat as proudly as the rest of them, but a bulkier man than most, was reading a newspaper in a large but elderly Pontiac which faced the front of the building.

Dawlish stared and winked at this particular chauffeur.

Ted Beresford winked back.

That was a heartening moment.

A porter who was dressed like a generalissimo in braid and medal ribbons asked Dawlish's pleasure, summoned a small boy who looked as if he was training to become a generalissimo, and despatched this small boy to accompany Dawlish to Bidot's apartment, on the fifth and top floor. That would be one of the most expensive apartments, for it would overlook most of the Bois de Boulogne, where it was possible to forget that one was in the heart of Paris.

Claire Bidot had often come in and out of here, and was now in the air raid shelter at home.

Simple?

Or very, very clever?

"It is this one," said the boy, and stopped in front of a door with pale blue and gilt scrollwork on it, and in a kind of gilded medallion, the number 53.

He pressed a bell.

"Fine, thanks," said Dawlish, and presented him with a five-hundred-franc note, much more than he could expect even from here, and said: "I'll be all right, now."

"M'sieur?"

"Allez toute suite," said Dawlish in execrable French, and the boy grinned and hurried off. He would not dream that this English giant could speak French almost as fluently as he could himself.

There was no sound, but the door opened; and Dawlish saw it moving, wondered if he would have any difficulty in seeing M. Bidot, who had obviously been frightened away from England so as to make sure he and Dawlish did not meet.

The door opened wider.

Blondie stood there.

"So you had to come," she said. She sounded almost weary, and yet looked scared as she moved to one side. One of the men whom Dawlish had handcuffed last night was just behind her. It was hardly surprising that he had a gun in his hand.

17 M. BIDOT

THERE WAS A MOMENT of absolute, electric silence. Then Dawlish relaxed very quickly, and beamed, and said:

"Hallo, Blondie, like a little cuddle?"

"You keep away from me!"

"And until last night you were following me all over the place," said Dawlish. "I can't understand women." He stepped inside, and the door was closed behind him quickly; but the girl didn't let him get too near, and even the fact that he had a gun didn't give the man much courage. "Still, it was smart to guess where I'd come next," Dawlish went on. "Is M. Bidot in?"

Blondie said, "Yes, he is."

"Fly in his own parlor," mused Dawlish. "Prisoner in his own house, or——"

Blondie said: "You talk too much. Go over there." She pointed to an open door, and from its position Dawlish judged that it led to a room which overlooked the Bois de Boulogne. He took a few steps toward it, eying Blondie, who still kept her distance.

She was quite a sight for the eye.

She wore a black suit, tight-fitting at the waist, full and unexpectedly decorous at the neckline. She had done her hair with great care this morning, and had made up very becomingly. Seen promenading in the rue St. Honoré or in the Place Vendôme she would have been quite a hit. She also had good legs, and was wearing tiny black patent shoes. While she led the way, the man with the gun stood to one side, keeping Dawlish covered all the time.

It was impossible to guess what to expect.

Bidot, in chains?

Bidot, also threatened by a gun?

Maidment?

Blondie opened the door, and Dawlish did not need telling why that was. She pushed the door wider open and stood aside for him to pass, and he said lightly:

"Stiff this morning?"

She didn't speak.

She looked at him rather oddly. It would not have surprised him had there been dislike in her expression, or even hatred, for she could not have enjoyed that bear-hugging session. Yet wariness was there, tinged, perhaps, with a kind of respect. Dawlish noted that and tucked it away in the back of his mind.

Then he stepped into a large, sunlit room, almost too obviously the room of a millionaire.

Standing with his back to the window was millionaire Bidot himself, alone and unfettered.

The door closed behind Dawlish, leaving these two men together.

Dawlish moved nearer to Bidot, whose back was toward the light and whose face, therefore, was in shadow. It was lean and aquiline. He had full, very pale lips and narrowed, pale gray eyes. There was strength in his face—and strength in his body, too. His shoulders were broad, and he stood much as a boxer might be when in repose. He was a long way from being as tall as Dawlish, but he was quite a man.

The surprising thing was his appearance.

Dawlish knew that he was in the middle forties. He looked much nearer thirty. There was not a hint of gray in the jet black hair, beautifully groomed, and hinting at a wave. There was not a sign of a line at his eyes or the corners of his mouth; nor at his forehead. He looked as if he had taken a course of rejuvenation which had been a complete success.

Dawlish waited for him to speak. He took a long time, and eyed Dawlish up and down, as if marveling at his strength and size, and yet determined that he should not be over impressed. There had been many curious situations since this affair had started, but none more curious than this.

Dawlish kept silent, too.

They eyed each other, so that it seemed almost as if it was going to be a childish test of who could outstare the other and who could wear down the other's patience first. Dawlish felt screaming curiosity, but outwardly he looked a little inane, smiling vaguely, and putting his head on one side. He could force this issue and make Bidot speak first, but—would that do any good? If this man saw himself as a kind of High Priest of Power, and if it would please him to have a minor triumph, why not give him that triumph?

Dawlish looked out of the window, and then into Bidot's face.

"Nice view," he remarked. "Nice day for it, too."

Then Bidot surprised him again, for he smiled. It was quite a performance. Until that moment he had kept his expression absolutely straight, there was no hint of a smile at lips or eyes; then suddenly his eyes crinkled at the corners, his lips curved, he showed a flash of white teeth. It might be turned off and on like a tap, but a lot of women were going to fall for a smile like that.

"So what I hear about you is true, Mr. Dawlish," he said.

"Don't know that I like the sound of that," said Dawlish warily. "Good? Bad?"

"That you have the supreme English characteristic of looking foolish when you're really very wise."

"Oh," said Dawlish. "I can't say that I see myself as an owl. Mind if I sit down?"

"Please do. Will you have a drink?"

"Do you know I don't mind if I do," said Dawlish. "It's a bit early, but five o'clock isn't too early in France, is it?" He watched as Bidot turned toward a magnificent walnut cocktail cabinet and pressed a button; the cabinet opened to reveal every alcoholic beverage in the book, and an array of cut glass which was almost worthy of a museum.

"What will you have?"

"Whiskey and soda, please."

Bidot's hand was very steady when he brought the drink to Dawlish. He did not drink himself, but drew back and sat on the arm of a three-seater settee which had probably cost a million francs. His light gray suit looked as if it had been molded to his body.

"Here's to health on the seven seas," said Dawlish, and drank. "May your life never be uncharted."

Bidot's smile came again.

"Your good health," he said dryly, and then raised his hands, the first Gallic gesture he had shown. "I think we must come to understand each other quickly, Mr. Dawlish. I have never believed that it was wise to waste time, or to hide facts. I made a mistake when I came to you in the first place, and I should not have given you those papers. May I have them, please?"

Dawlish had never seen him before, in the flesh.
He knew nothing about any papers.
This was a quietly spoken lie.
Like wife, like husband.

"As you were saying, we have to understand each other quickly," Dawlish said. "What papers?"

"I hope you aren't going to persist in an attitude of ignorance," said Bidot. "My wife gave them to you, a few days ago. At the time, I thought that I needed your help. Circumstances have changed. I admit that the changes have been forced on me, but"—he shrugged, hands rising again—"a wise man does not refuse to accept a reverse. May I have the papers, please?"

He knew that this was nonsense.

Or else he believed his wife had given those papers to Dawlish.

No man in his senses would behave like this without a good reason; the essential thing now was to find out what that reason was. Take the obvious possibility, Dawlish decided. The others were listening, they might even be watching; in walls as ornate as these, it would be comparatively easy to have a peephole. Bidot knew that his wife had not given any papers to Dawlish; so he was trying to make sure that the others believed that he had.

It wouldn't matter if Dawlish denied it.

Would it help if he admitted it?

Bidot's back was to the door, and Dawlish was facing him. The huge window, with its beautiful view, could not hide anyone; so, his expression could not be seen. Nor could the way he mouthed "Admit that you have them" very carefully. He had hardly stopped before he went on again in a rather touchier voice:

"Why waste time? Where are the papers, Mr. Dawlish?"

"I don't think you quite understand the situation," Dawlish responded clearly. "Even if I knew where they were, I wouldn't hand them over now. I might hand them over in exchange for my wife."

He beamed.

Anyone listening might well construe that into an admission that he knew where the papers were. The slight easing in Bidot's expression suggested that it was as much as he had hoped for.

"That is impossible," Bidot said curtly.

"Who was it who said that the impossible took a little longer than the difficult?" asked Dawlish mildly; but the expression in his eyes wasn't mild, and his voice began to harden, for the benefit of anyone who might be listening in this room. "First I want my wife. After that, I might talk business."

"It will have to be the other way around," Bidot said flatly. "And you haven't much time, Dawlish." He dropped the courtesy "Mr." for the first time as he stood up from the arm of the couch and went to a cabinet in the corner of the lovely room. His footsteps made no sound at all on the thick carpet, and he moved with grace and with distinction; he was a good match for Claire.

"I think I'll have to explain a little more in the bargain, and perhaps that will help to convince you. First about the papers. I have a world-wide fleet of merchant vessels, as you know, and a smaller fleet of pleasure craft—small steam yachts which take parties of thirty or forty on extensive cruises. I have my own steam yacht, too. You may think that this gives me everything I need, but there is one thing it doesn't give me, because in Europe it is impossible to get. That is security and peace of mind. There is no peace left in Europe, or the Middle East, or the Far East. We are continually at the mercy of events. My ships, for instance, might be held up in Australia because of a strike, in Chinese ports because of incidents, in the Middle East because some band of marauding nationalists has holed an oil pipeline. You see what I mean?"

"You could read it in any newspaper article," Dawlish said, and wondered what was coming next.

"That is true. But so many people read a newspaper article, marvel or are shocked, and then turn to the sporting pages and forget world events. I don't behave quite like that. I don't relish being at the mercy of world events, which are dictated by fanatics or fools, and seldom by wise men. So, some three years ago, I decided to take steps against being victimized by world events. I sent or took security, in the guise of gold, jewels, *objets d'art*, to many places of the world. Few are in Europe, few in the Far East. Most are in the Americas, the West Indies, parts of Africa, islands in many places including the South Seas. Wherever I was forced to go, I believed, I would have all that I needed. In other words I took out a form of insurance, and had these—these goods delivered not to one or two but to fifty different places in the world. I did not send them to banks and safety deposits, which would be raided at once by any hostile invaders. I used less likely places. I made a list, in code, giving all details of valuables and the hiding places. The missing papers include all this. There is no other record. Each package, each crate, was taken by a different ship with a different crew, and only one man then living knew what I was doing. No one at all knew where I had put these insurances for my future."

Bidot paused.

Dawlish had been held almost fascinated by the story and by the way it was told, with Bidot standing close to that cabinet of polished wood, and speaking very quietly. As he paused, his expression changed, he looked like a man who had suffered a grievous hurt.

He went on:

"That one man was a lifelong business associate whose

name was Maurice Dillon. I told him what I was doing, but not where the different crates were stored. I now know that between us we made one important mistake. We had as a doctor on our staff an Englishman, one Claude Maidment, who served on several ships and for several cruises over a number of years. He observed these crates and packages going to the different places and noticed that all of them had identical markings—my code markings. Unknown to us, he and two members of the crew of a vessel went to the hold, several months ago, broke open a crate, and found inside the valuables—gold, precious stones, various currencies.

"Maidment quickly guessed the rest.

"He knew six of the places where similar crates were stored, but did not know exactly where they were kept. He also guessed that there might be sixty. He set to work to find out, using a young woman you now know—this Blondie." Bidot shrugged, and even managed to smile. "Maurice fell in love with her, and even when he knew what she wanted, he could not bring himself to get rid of her, or tell me. He told her of the existence of the coded list. Soon afterward" —Bidot was talking in a husky voice, with his eyes half closed, as if the recollection pained him—"Maurice was drowned when a small yacht foundered. The crew of two escaped, and I know that these men served Maidment. He has, in all, seven or eight sailors in his pay, and once he has the list he proposes to charter a small vessel, and go around and collect these stores of mine. For those papers include authority to allow anyone presenting them to collect the hidden stores."

After a long pause, Dawlish said slowly:

"And you intend to let him collect?"

"I shall have to," Bidot said simply. "He has all the trumps. I did not know this until yesterday. He and the blonde girl learned more from Maurice than I have told you. In my early days, I committed a crime, a simple one of the evasion of taxation. I confess to you that I did this on a large scale. Today, I would not do so, but"—he shrugged his shoulders—"it is a fact that money and possessions can create the desire for more and more money and possessions, and not many years ago I was a victim of my own success. Maidment discovered that, and has the proof. Unless I let him do what he wishes, he will use that proof. I prefer that it should not be used, Dawlish. When I first saw you, I did not know about this. I knew that Maurice's death was difficult to explain, I knew that I was being threatened—blackmailed by telephone—and I didn't know why. I knew that Maurice had told someone about these papers, so—I gave them to you." Bidot paused at that just long enough for Dawlish to break in if he wished to, but Dawlish kept silent. "After I had done so, I realized that I was quite defenseless. As you know, I wanted you to find out what was behind all this, and to help me. Now, I know. If I had any doubts about what I was to do, such doubts vanished when Maidment—whom I had believed to be a friend—took my wife away. I stand to lose my wife, whom I love, and my fortune, which I value, and my reputation, which I cherish," Bidot went on in an even voice. "I have not the courage to lose any one of these. So I will give up the papers and all they mean. Among other advantages, I should get back the proofs of my earlier frauds. After all,"—his lips twisted wryly as he went on—"I can always start again, selecting different hiding places, and using a different doctor."

He stopped.

Dawlish said: "Perhaps Maidment's hand isn't as strong as it seems."

"Oh, indeed it is," said Bidot, in his curiously precise English. "It is an impregnable position from all points of view. When he knew that I had gotten in touch with you, he found out all he could about you. You have a very great reputation, you know. He realized that in some ways you might be more dangerous than I. You would have less to lose, and would not necessarily be so jealous of my reputation or possessions. You know how he took your wife away, and so demonstrated his resourcefulness. And he gave himself a weapon against you which you dare not let him use.

"I know Maidment very well, Dawlish.

"I know that he will kill if it suits his purpose, and I know that he does not threaten in vain.

"He has your wife. I do not know where she is; he made sure that I could not find out. He also made sure that I knew how helpless she was."

Dawlish felt his tension rising, felt his hands clenching. The slow, quiet way in which Bidot moved and spoke was infuriating.

Bidot opened the cabinet, and revealed that it was a tape recorder. He pressed a switch, and the recorder began to turn around slowly. He faced Dawlish, and said:

"This is what convinced me, and on his instructions I am to play it back to you, so that you know the position. It is a conversation between your wife and her captors, taken only a few hours ago. I—I use the word conversation, Dawlish, but it is both more and less than that. I must warn you to be prepared for——"

He stopped.

He pressed a switch. . . .

Felicity's voice came into the room, crying:

"No! No, take it away, take it away!"

She was on the edge of terror.

18 TRANSCRIPTION

"No! No, TAKE IT AWAY, *take it away!*"

It was impossible to guess what "it" was, possible only to be sure that the voice was Felicity's, and that she was badly frightened. Dawlish moved slowly and stiffly toward the cabinet, staring at the revolving wheels and the tape, which was momentarily silent; his jaw was set so tightly that it hurt.

A man said: "Don't you like snakes, then?"

He spoke quietly and sneeringly, and it was a voice which Dawlish could not remember hearing before; and he went on:

"Come on, Salem, get back into your box, the lady doesn't like you." There followed silence except for a faint rustling and a sound which seemed to get louder and louder; as if someone was breathing very harshly and agitatedly. It was easy to believe that it was Felicity, staring at the snake coiling itself into a box or a basket, hardly knowing how to stand erect while the thing was loose.

Then: "You had better hope your husband is reasonable, Mrs. Dawlish."

The only answer was in that harsh breathing; evidence of Felicity's fear.

"You'd better hope that he does exactly what we want him to do, or you won't see him again. Did you ever see a film called *The Snake Pit?*"

Felicity was panting for breath.

"Did you ever see a snake pit?" asked the man sneeringly. "Did you ever think what it would be like to have a dozen of these little pets crawling over your body and——"

"*No!*"

"Your nerves aren't so good, are they?" asked the man, and his voice was cold and dispassionate and somehow ugly and menacing. "I can't understand it, you haven't been with us long. How about sending a littte message to your dear husband, Mrs. Dawlish?"

Felicity made no response.

"You'd better," the man went on in a harder voice, "because you'll never get away from here unless you do. You'll never get off the——"

There was a sharp break in the recording, as if the

130

speaker had broken off abruptly, or else a piece had been cut out, and the tape re-joined. "You'll never get off the——" held a clue that might be vital, and it registered on Dawlish's mind in spite of everything that was happening to him, in spite of the tensions and the fears.

"—and don't forget it. You'd better ask Dawlish to hand those papers over quickly."

There was no answer; just Felicity's tense and terrible breathing.

"Don't tell me you've lost your tongue," the man sneered.

That was when Felicity spoke.

That was also the longest moment in Dawlish's life. For his Felicity, his wife, spoke at last. Her voice was unsteady and some of the words were slurred, but what she said was clear enough for anyone to hear.

"It won't make any difference what I say to him," she said. "He'll do whatever he has to do. You'll never frighten him."

That was all.

The spool came slowly to a standstill, leaving the lovely room in utter silence.

Dawlish took out a handkerchief and dabbed at his forehead, and found that the handkerchief was almost wet through. He did not know how pale he was, could not tell how tightly his hands and his teeth were clenched. He saw the way Bidot looked at him, and it was almost as if Bidot were frightened.

The silence dragged on.

No one came in, no door opened, there was no sound of movement until Bidot pressed the switch again and the cabinet closed. Then he took a step forward, hesitated, changed direction and went to the cocktail cabinet. He poured out a strong whiskey, splashed soda, and carried the drink to Dawlish.

"Drink this," he said abruptly.

131

Dawlish stared into his eyes.

"Drink it!"

"Ah," said Dawlish. "Thanks." He took the glass and tossed the whiskey and soda down as if it were water on a hot day, and then he banged the glass onto a small table. "Where is she?"

"I do not know."

"*Where is she?*"

"I tell you that I do not know. Return the papers, and Maidment will——"

"If you don't tell me where my wife is, I'll break your neck," Dawlish said, and took a step closer to the Frenchman, his hands stretched outward, the fingers crooked as if he wanted to get them tight about Bidot's neck. "You know all right."

He saw fear in Bidot's face.

Dawlish would have strangled anyone who got in his way, so great was his fury, so completely was he lost to reason. Then he heard sounds behind him; the door opening, men moving, men ringing him, as they might a dangerous animal, men with guns. There were two whom he had seen before, and a third he thought he had seen, a man of medium height, middle-aged, balding, perhaps a little too plump and a little too smug. As he stared, Dawlish remembered seeing him in Brighton.

This wasn't the aquiline-featured man of the previous night, whose profile had shown up so vividly, when he had thought it might be Maidment.

He did not carry a weapon, but seemed to rely on the guns in the hands of the two other men. Bidot was now behind Dawlish, as if he no longer mattered.

"When I have the papers," the plumpish man said in a smooth, plummy English voice, "you can have your wife. Until then, you won't see her again. Why don't you stop making it difficult, Dawlish? I know you have the papers."

The truth was that Bidot was trying to save himself by pretending that Dawlish had the papers.

Dawlish made himself stand there and work that out; he made himself reject the impulse to rush at these men and smash their heads together. He might reach them, might even injure them before they shot him, but that wouldn't help Felicity. What mattered was helping her, and he could not, because he did not know where the papers were.

And they would not believe him.

Bidot must know where to find them.

So he had to make Bidot tell him.

Maidment spoke again, still plummily. He was a man who might be seen in London or any English town with a bowler hat and a neat, dark serge suit, well-polished shoes. He would get out of a small family car, he would carry *The Times* or the *Telegraph*, he would watch cricket matches whenever he could, and spend a few Saturday afternoons at Twickenham during the winter. That was Dr. Maidment, and there were tens of thousands of men like him; but only this one knew where Felicity was.

"You're just banging your head against a brick wall, Dawlish," he said. "Bidot was doing that until I made him see reason."

Presumably the final turn of the screw had been when Bidot's wife had been kidnapped. "My wife, whom I love very much." There was a key, perhaps; there was the lead which Dawlish was looking for. If only he could think clearly, get the rage out of his mind, get rid of the burning desire to crack the heads of these men together until their skulls splintered. He was in better control of himself, now; his mind was really beginning to work again.

He could not work against Maidment yet.

The only hope of finding out where Felicity was lay in those papers.

Once he had them, he could bargain with Maidment. He

couldn't do a thing until he had them, and Bidot knew where they were.

Bidot was in love with his wife.

And his wife was in the old air raid shelter beneath Four Ways.

All of them were watching Dawlish closely, and the men with the automatics were poised to shoot if he made an aggressive move. Even Blondie was here now, standing closer to the door in that unbelievably decorous black outfit. Lover of Maurice, who had been drowned by "accident" and yet had been murdered.

Maidment began again:

"No one need get hurt, Dawlish. This is a matter of arrangement between sensible people. Bidot has already acknowledged that. You can't get anywhere by behaving like a bull in a china shop. Now, hand over the papers, and let's get the whole thing finished."

He was frowning, rather impatiently, as if rain threatened at Lord's, that mecca of cricket, and the batsmen were taking an unconscionable time getting the runs needed to win.

Dawlish said softly: "By all means, let the voice of reason speak. Let's be calm, cool and calculating. Bidot, you start. Did you know that Maidment lost your wife last night? He sent her to try to make me tell her where the papers were, but it didn't work out that way. I have her, quite safe. Safe, that is, at the moment."

Now he would know how much Bidot's wife meant to the man.

19 CALLER

HAD BIDOT KNOWN ALREADY what had happened to Claire?

Dawlish, watching him closely, felt sure that he had not

134

been told. First astonishment, then disbelief showed on his face, and he looked sharply at Maidment.

"Why don't you stop lying?" Maidment asked, more roughly than he had yet spoken. "Do you think I'd let a thing like that happen, Bidot?"

Bidot looked at Dawlish.

At last Dawlish was smiling; at last he saw a way of exerting pressure which would make sure that Bidot told him where those papers were. Danger to his Claire affected him as much as danger to Felicity affected Dawlish. That was wonderful; that was the course of true love!

". . . listen to the liar!" Maidment was saying.

Dawlish's smile was almost fatuous. Maidment was scowling. Bidot wasn't yet sure whom to believe, but for the first time that outward show of composure was cracking.

"Well, well," Dawlish said, "Maidment forgot to tell you that I spirited Claire away last night and his bonny boys couldn't find her. Before they had a chance, the police arrived and sent them packing. Who was the man in charge last night, Maidment?"

"Don't believe him!" Maidment snapped.

"The interesting thing about this situation is that we all have our weak spots," said Dawlish amiably. "I needn't tell you about mine. Your wife isn't unimportant to you, Bidot, and who could forget your money and your reputation? And now we've found your weak spot, Doctor. You daren't tell Bidot the truth, and while I have Claire and the papers are still missing, you can't do much."

Maidment was glowering at him.

"Well, it's a nice evening," said Dawlish. "I think I'll go for a little stroll in the Bois. Coming, Blondie?" He beamed at the girl. "I promise not to do more than squeeze your hand." He moved toward the door, covered by the automatics, knowing that both Bidot and Maidment were momentarily beaten; but this was a brittle kind of triumph, there would be no real triumph until he knew where Felicity was, and could bring her to safety.

"No! No, take it away, take it away!"
And the man's voice:
"You'll never get off the———"
The what?

"If you don't give me those papers . . ." Maidment began.

Dawlish thumbed his nose at the doctor as he reached the door. The two gunmen stood aside; they might shoot him, they wouldn't readily allow him to get within arm's reach.

"I think I shall stay at the Carlton," Dawlish said. "Inquire there if any of you want to see me."

He could step through the doorway.

Blondie had backed away, and stood between them and the passage door, a little scared, but looking very different from what he had expected. The two men could shoot at a word from Maidment, but Maidment believed that Dawlish had the papers, and there was no other way of getting them. The odds were that he would not be shot.

"Incidentally," he said, "you haven't seen those friends of mine here, have you? Friends of friends, perhaps, would be more accurate. Superintendent William Trivett has a pal or two at the *Sûreté Nationale,* don't be too surprised if the *gendarmerie* cluster around if I fail to show up before long. Or do I mean *agents de police?* Good evening, gentlemen. Hi, Toots." He moved swiftly, and actually chucked Blondie under the chin. "What a nice girl you'd have been with the proper friends."

She stood to one side, half smiling at him, and now he recognized the expression in her eyes; one of reluctant admiration. He'd seen that kind of expression often enough to recognize it. He knew now that he would be allowed to go out of the apartment without difficulty, but his major problem was still to find out where Felicity was. He did not think he would be able to frighten anyone here into telling him, but he might find a clue if he could turn the tables on them for ten minutes.

Was there even half a chance?

Would Blondie——

There was a sharp ringing sound, and he knew that it was the front door, for Blondie looked at it quickly. He glanced around in turn. The men looked alarmed, as if the call was a surprise to them; and after his talk of the police, they might be really scared. He hadn't talked of the police last night, but they had arrived.

"See who it is, Blondie," Dawlish ordered.

She looked for permission to Maidment.

"Don't move," Maidment said sharply. "Dawlish, you wait until they go away."

"How very discourteous of you," said Dawlish, in a loud clear voice. "Would it be better if you let them think you— or M. Bidot—was in his bath? That's if he sings in his bath. Idy Ho!" he yodeled, throwing his head back and making a noise which could probably be heard down in the heart of the Bois de Boulogne itself. "Danny, where are you?" He chucked Blondie under the chin again, and then said: "Very well, I shall open the door. Maidment, if the police are outside, I shouldn't think they would approve of your men shooting. Hotel Carlton, and don't be too long, I'm in a mood to talk terms."

He opened the door.

Ted Beresford stood there.

Dawlish should have expected him, he should have made allowances for the fact that Ted would not let him stay here too long. He had forgotten his own strength in reckoning the weakness of the others.

Ted looked enormous as he stood waiting, and his homely face showed the extent of his relief.

"Hallo, Pat."

"Hi, Ted," said Dawlish. "Just stay in the passage for a moment, will you? If you hear shooting, run hell for leather for the lift, and send the police. The interested parties are a Dr. Maidment, presumably with an English passport, a M. Bidot, known as a millionaire, and a girl named Blondie. With curves. Also, two assorted men with guns. Did you bring your gun?"

"One for each hand," said Beresford. His eyes were smiling, and he didn't turn a hair in spite of Dawlish's burbling. "Glad to have a chance to use 'em."

"Hear that?" asked Dawlish, and turned around to face the others. He was still beaming. Blondie was near him, the two men with the automatics were near the communicating door, and Maidment and Bidot were almost tight into the doorway. "Nothing is ever what it seems, dear Doctor, is it?" He moved forward, past Blondie, up to the two startled men. He held a hand out toward each. Pistols, please. Don't use them, because the police certainly wouldn't take long to get here."

He thrust a hand in front of each of them.

Each darted an almost piteous glance toward Maidment, who didn't speak or give them a lead of any kind. Then they placed their automatics in Dawlish's hands.

"Thank you, gentlemen," said Dawlish with a vast smile. "Now, go over to that wall near Blondie, and take everything out of your pockets. Blondie, you too. Bidot, do you know where Maidment is staying in Paris?"

Bidot didn't speak.

"Doctor dear," cooed Dawlish, "let's see what you carry about with you, too. I just want to go and have a look at your apartment or hotel room, in case you've left my wife's address." He sounded almost flippant as he said that. "Incidentally, if my wife should get hurt, I shall take you to pieces. Small pieces. Slowly. Now, empty your pockets."

138

Nothing on these men revealed where Felicity was.

But Maidment had keys and cards, and the cards gave his address at an apartment near St. Germain des Prés, on the left bank of the Seine.

"Not too bad," said Dawlish, when he had discovered this, and he felt nearer light-hearted than he had all day. "Blondie, do you know where the larder is? Or would the bathroom be a better bet?"

"I don't know what you mean," Blondie said, but there was a hint of a smile in her lovely eyes.

"Just a cupboard or a closet where we can lock all of you up. I don't want to be interrupted while I'm at Maidment's apartment. Any preference?"

"When Dr. Maidment gets out of this, he'll make you wish——" Blondie began.

"Don't finish!" exclaimed Dawlish. "It's been said far too often over the years." He glanced at Ted Beresford, who had been inspecting the apartment. "What's the best place, Ted?"

"Bathroom. No window," Ted said.

"Lady and gentlemen," Dawlish urged, "all into the bathroom, please."

It was nearly half past six when Dawlish and Beresford reached the front of the apartment building. The generalissimo was still there, and he saluted; the boy training to step into his uniform smiled broadly at Dawlish. The hired car was where he had left it, among the evidences of opulence in gay colors and bright chromium.

"Still got your car?" Dawlish asked.

"That old Pontiac over there."

"Good. I'll lead the way," Dawlish said. "Where's Joan?"

"Window shopping."

"Sure she's not here?"

"Sure as I can be."

"Fine," said Dawlish. "I'll tell you more about it when we get to Maidment's place."

"Oke," Ted said.

He walked to the Pontiac rather slowly, limping a little. In fact he had an artificial leg, having lost a leg in a job on which he and Dawlish had been working, years ago. Many people who thought they knew Beresford well were unaware of this. He got into his car as Dawlish started the engine of the Citroën. No one took any especial interest in them, and Dawlish moved into the main road and then into the flood of the Paris evening traffic. It seemed wild to dart in all directions at once; tiny cars and wasp-like Vespas roared and screeched and purred their way to the heart of Paris or the suburbs. The journey to St. Germain des Prés took nearly three-quarters of an hour.

Dawlish arrived first.

The apartment was in a house approached, like most of the houses here, through a small door in large wooden doors which led to a cobbled courtyard. A *concierge* sat inside a small room, with a copy of *France-Soir* open in front of him. Dawlish nodded, and went to the doorway leading to the staircase, which wound up and up four or five stories. Dawlish walked up. Beresford would find it heavier going, but he would make it.

On the second floor, there was a visiting card over a doorbell, which said: "Dr. C. P. Maidment."

Claude Maidment?

Dawlish used Maidment's key. It turned easily in the lock. He pushed the door open an inch, and listened intently. There was no sound. Maidment might have a wife here, a mistress, a servant. He could afford to take nothing for granted.

Beresford came into sight.

Dawlish raised a hand to him, and then stepped into the apartment. Curtains were drawn at all the windows, and the place was gloomy and dark. For a few wild moments Dawlish wondered if Felicity could be here; but she was not. No one was, although there was a man's bedroom as well as a woman's. Blondie's?

Beresford joined Dawlish.

They began a search of the apartment which was as thorough as Trivett could have made with two Yard experts. Bureaus, dressing-table drawers, drawers everywhere, any place where documents might be kept, were thoroughly searched; but Dawlish found nothing that helped. He kept thinking of the way that man on the tape recorder had broken off. *Off*: that was the key word. You would say out of a house, but off an island, of course. Out of a house, out of a country, off a ship, off an island.

He told Ted all that mattered of what had happened. Ted grunted occasionally, moved slowly, and went on methodically with his search. Somewhere not far away Joan was window shopping and, undoubtedly, worrying. Not far away, Dorothy Jeremy was probably window shopping and wishing she was helping Dawlish. Somewhere unknown, Felicity——

"Off," Ted interjected abruptly. "Off a ship, off an island. English Channel, presumably."

"What have you found?" asked Dawlish.

"Deed of Sale, little island in the Channel Islands, called Silla," Ted said, and held the document up. "Might be interesting. House or two there, tiny harbor, the usual. About fifteen miles off the French coast, according to this diagram. Most northerly of the islands, so not very far from Brighton. Want a look?"

Dawlish took the document, and felt his heart thumping, felt that he was being choked. He saw the diagram, the sketch of the position of the island in relation to the larger ones in the group, and believed that they had found the answer to the question: where was Felicity imprisoned?

Then, the telephone bell rang.

They were in a living room. The telephone, an old-fashioned, spidery-looking affair, was on a table near the door. They were by a bureau standing in the tall windows. Dawlish looked around. Ted Beresford sniffed, and said:

"Better let it ring, hadn't we?"

Dawlish said: "I don't know." He went across to it, and the bell kept ringing, as if the caller meant to make sure that he was answered. It went on and on and on, until at last Dawlish took off the receiver. He spoke in French, and with an accent that seemed perfect; this was the residence of M. le Médicin—M. Maidment.

A woman said, as if startled: "Who's that?"

The two words were enough to tell him that this was Blondie, and that his accent had fooled her. He did not think that Blondie would be ringing just to say hallo, and he dropped into English quickly.

"Hallo, Blondie, what's on? Dawlish here."

"A man came and let them out, and they're on their way," Blondie said abruptly, and she could hardly get the words out, she was so breathless. "Papers or no papers, they won't let you get away again. Maidment's just told the others to kill you at all cost."

Without another word, she rang off.

20 SENT TO KILL

BLONDIE HADN'T NEEDED to say any more.

Maidment would know that Dawlish would find the deed and would be sure that the Isle of Silla was the place he wanted. And once Dawlish got there and found his wife, or if he alerted the Channel Island Police and sent a search party to the island, he, Maidment, would never have a chance.

So, he would send his men to kill, and he would come to kill himself.

Ted said dryly, "Better look slippy, hadn't we?"

"Put that back where you found it," Dawlish said. "He might be fooled into thinking we haven't seen it." He moved toward the front door, and opened it an inch; there was no sound. It was impossible to be sure how much time he had to spare, but it had taken a long time to get here from Bidot's place, and with luck there was still enough.

Ted came, hurrying clumsily.

"I'll go first," Dawlish said. "Don't take any chances if they shoot."

Ted gave a quick, homely grin.

"Shoot first, Pat, don't worry. Quite like old times," he added calmly, and there was a glint in his eyes as he came out of the apartment. "You hurry. I might hold us both up."

"In a minute I shall carry you," Dawlish said.

Beresford brushed his heavy dark hair back from his forehead, and said:

"Mind out of the way while I jump."

They were silent from then on, except when Beresford made a faint sound as he went down. Dawlish reached the cobbled yard some distance ahead, and opened the door a few inches, peering out. No one was in sight, and the small door set in the large wooden door which led to the street was closed. He stepped outside. The *concierge* still sat in front of his newspaper with a pair of rimless glasses on, pretending to read. Beresford reached the ground floor, and Dawlish went across the courtyard.

Beresford was at the door, and Dawlish close to the small wooden door, when a man stepped through.

He was not from Bidot's apartment, and Dawlish hadn't seen him before, but he was sallow and lithe and very much like the men who worked for Maidment. He came in stealthily, too, and his right hand was in his pocket.

He saw Dawlish, and stopped abruptly.

"Look out!" Ted whispered, from behind Dawlish.

Dawlish needed no telling. There was the split second while the man in the doorway stared—and then Dawlish saw a slight movement inside his pocket, and had no doubt that the other was going to shoot through the cloth. Dawlish flung himself to one side. As he did so, he heard the muffled report of the shot. Then Beresford gasped, and Dawlish knew that he had been hit.

Dawlish leapt forward.

The little man who had shot Beresford fired again, but he was panicky, and the bullet smacked into the cobbles by Dawlish's side. But Dawlish had no chance to stop him from going out, and he could wait in the street and shoot as Dawlish stepped through.

There was just one thing to do.

Dawlish shot at him.

He shot at the thigh. He did not reckon on the man slipping and falling. He did not reckon on the bullet smacking into the skull, with a strange, thudding sound; or on the way the man collapsed.

Dawlish stood quite still for a moment that was horror-filled. But he dared not let it stop him, and he turned.

"Ted——"

"Get away," Beresford gasped. "I'm all—all right. Get away!"

He had a wound in the shoulder, and already blood was showing at the opening of his shirt. He was leaning against the wall, off balance, and wouldn't be able to hurry. It would be impossible to help him and get away with any hope of reaching Felicity. If once Dawlish was held by the police, all chance would be gone. All these thoughts flashed through his mind as he tried to decide what to do. Why not wait, tell the police, hope that they would take action, and——

Time was the essence of all this.

There would be the sensation here, questions, delays, doctors and ambulance. It would be half an hour or more before he was taken away. Then there would be more questions, from a magistrate probably. No one would believe him, for his story would sound preposterous. At best he could expect to make a call to Trivett at the Yard in two hours or so, almost certainly too late.

Beresford cried: *"Look out!"*

Dawlish spun around.

The old *concierge* was opening the door of his room, and he carried a shotgun. At sight of Dawlish he jumped back and let the door slam on him; but he could fire through the window, and might be able to stop Dawlish from getting away.

Dawlish covered him with his gun.

He saw the telephone by the *concierge*'s right hand, and could be sure that the police had already been called. He backed swiftly toward the door, but had to be wary. He glimpsed the blood which was beginning to ooze from the dead man's skull. He opened the little door, as the *concierge* took his courage in both hands and came into the open again.

"Stop that!" Beresford shouted.

Dawlish stepped into the street, and pulled the little wooden door behind him. This was a one-way street, with cars parked on one side only—and his was twenty yards away, Beresford's a little farther on. He strode toward it. A woman carrying some milk bottles was stepping out of a tiny grocery store and jumped back out of his way. A young couple, looking into a window, stared in amazement. From farther along, where he had just come from, there was shouting and bellowing. Dawlish reached his hired car, wrenched open the door and climbed in. He couldn't understand how Bidot's man had arrived here so quickly, unless it had been some time before Blondie had been able to get to the telephone. He turned the key and pressed the self-starter in one and the same movement—and nothing happened.

He pressed again.

He knew, on that instant, that the car had been tampered with. He tried twice again, but there was no whisper of response. Getting out, he noticed that the hood was raised a little. He flung it up, and he saw what had happened; the distributor head had been taken away; until it was back, nothing could make the car go.

Ted's?

Dawlish hurried toward the other car as a police car appeared, with three policemen standing on the running board. So soon? Two others appeared on foot, at a corner; Ted's car was just beyond the corner. Dawlish reached it, but its hood was up, too. So someone had been watching Maidment's apartment, had seen him and Ted arrive, and made sure they couldn't get away.

Dawlish moved.

Two more policemen came hurrying from the other direction. They did not look at him, but it would not be long before every *gendarme* and *agent* in Paris would be on the lookout for a huge Englishman; and his was a stature and face which could not be disguised.

A taxi came along, its flag showing *Libre*. That might mean anything or nothing in a Paris taxi. Dawlish waved. The taxi pulled in toward him, and a heavily built taxi driver gave him a surly: *"M'sieur?"*

Where to?

Dawlish said: "Bois de Boulogne. *Apartements des Hautes."*

If this cabby didn't want to go in that direction he would shrug and shake his head.

He nodded.

Dawlish got in. He thought he heard a commotion behind him, but didn't look around. The cabby, sleepy-eyed and drowsy-looking until then, seemed to wake up. He hurled the car forward toward the next traffic lights as if it was a matter of life and death that he should beat everything behind. He did. Two or three little Renaults, a Volkswagen and a small Austin were coming along behind, but no police cars.

Dawlish leaned back and closed his eyes, then lit a cigarette. It wasn't easy to get the sight of that dead man out of his mind's eye. Death was an ugly thing. He himself would have been killed, but . . .

Brooding wouldn't help.

Dawlish tossed the half-finished cigarette out of the window. The taxi, twenty years old at least, went along like a greyhound on crutches, every now and again showing a turn of speed which would have been alarming at any other time. The journey which had taken Dawlish forty minutes took this old wreck barely twenty; and the driver was as surly at the end of it as he had been at the beginning.

Dawlish put a five-thousand franc note into his hand, and turned away. He heard the man shout:

"M'sieur!" Eyes blazed, the note waved. *"Une mille, m'sieur, c'est trop. . . ."*

"Keep it," Dawlish said, and hurried into the building. He did just discern the disbelief in the taxi driver's eye. The generalissimo was talking to a duchess, and the smaller version was nowhere in sight. Dawlish took himself up in the lift. At the top floor he kept a hand around his gun as he stepped toward Bidot's apartment. He was not going to forget the dead man in a hurry.

The door was closed.

Dawlish rang the bell. There was a pause, he rang again sharply, and the door opened. For the second time, Blondie stood there to greet him, but this time she looked astounded.

"Who is it?" Bidot called out.

Dawlish said: "Dawlish," and stepped in and closed the door behind him. "Thanks for the warning," he said. "There was trouble but I've scraped out of it. Bidot, how much does your wife mean to you?"

Bidot was in the doorway, broad and yet elegant; and very tense.

"Everything," he said, with quiet vehemence.

"We're lucky in our wives," Dawlish said. "I want to get to the Isle of Silla, just as fast as we can. Know it?"

"The Isle of Silla!" Bidot cried.

"Do you know it?"

"It was the first of the islands that I used. It——" Bidot broke off, and moved forward hurriedly. "Is that where your wife is?"

"I think so. How long will it take us?"

Bidot said: "We can drive to the airport, and be at Le Havre in half an hour. An hour and a half from then we can be at the island. I have a fast motorboat at Le Havre."

"Is it ready to move off?"

"It is always kept in readiness."

"I've just one job to do first," Dawlish said, and lifted the telephone. "If you have a gun or anything lethal, I'd take it." He changed from English to French on the instant, speaking into the telephone. "I want to call London, please, quickly."

He paused again.

Then he gave the number of Scotland Yard. Blondie, now alone with him, for Bidot was in another room, raised her head sharply. He waited for what seemed an age, and Bidot came back, carrying a small automatic.

The operator said: "I regret the delay is one hour."

"I'll send a telegram," Dawlish said, abruptly.

Bidot and Blondie were now at the door. Dawlish stood sweating with impatience, until another operator answered. He sent the telegram to Trivett, saying: "Felicity at Isle of Silla Channel Islands situation desperate," and rang off. He turned around and spared a moment to look into Blondie's

148

eyes. "Sorry," he said. "Blondie, take care of yourself. If Maidment finds out what you did, he won't like it."

"I daren't let Maidment catch me again," Blondie said, in a steady voice. She met his gaze. "I made an excuse not to leave here with him. I just can't go on, always lying, thieving, cheating. I just can't. But he'll kill me as he'll kill you, because he hasn't a chance while any of us are alive. He'll come back here if he didn't leave men to watch for you in case you came."

Dawlish was already heading for the door.

"If you mean you want to come too, get a move on," he said, and reached the door. But he did not open it too quickly; he was very cautious, and peered outside intently. No one was in the passage. He opened the door wider, and the others joined him, without speaking; Bidot closed the door. "Is there a back way out?" asked Dawlish.

"There is an emergency exit, and a service lift," answered Bidot. "This way."

They went down in the small service lift, and when they reached the bottom, Dawlish went out cautiously, as he had upstairs. No one but two surprised maids noticed them. He led the way around the side of the big building, still walking very stealthily. He reached a corner and looked around, toward the generalissimo and the duchess, the plutocrats' cars, the flowers and the shrubs, the lawns—and two of Maidment's men. He was quite sure who they were.

They went into the building.

"Which is your car?" asked Dawlish.

"The silver-gray Rolls-Bentley."

"You'd better drive, you know the road better than I," Dawlish said. He headed for the Rolls-Bentley, Bidot in front of him. Bidot opened the door for Blondie, as if there was all the time in the world. But he slammed the door after her and hurried.

Dawlish sat in the back with the girl.

149

"Bidot, we couldn't be in a greater hurry," he said quietly. "Maidment left a man behind, at his apartment, and he nearly put paid to Beresford and me. That was before he got badly hurt. Half Paris is on the lookout for me."

Bidot was reversing out of the parking place.

"It will be impossible to drive more quickly than I," he said calmly. "Did the man die?"

"Yes."

"It cannot be helped. I hope that if we find your wife in time, you will not inform the police of what I told you," Bidot said quietly, but there was nothing gentle about the way he shot the Rolls-Bentley forward. "It is possible that when he knows he cannot get what he wants, Maidment will say nothing, hoping to blackmail me again."

"If we find my wife, I don't care a damn whether the police get on to you or not," Dawlish said. "I'll keep silent and you'll get your wife back, provided you really try to reach the Isle of Silla."

"You will see," said Bidot.

Blondie was sitting very still next to Dawlish. He knew that she was looking at him. He felt her hand move, and take his. There was nothing seductive about it; in a strange way it was like a child taking his hand, as if for comfort. She smiled in a twisted sort of way.

"What do you have to do, to be loved like you love your wife?" she asked. "It never happened to me."

Dawlish looked at her for a long time, then smiled and said:

"You just have to be lucky."

"Thank you for that," said Blondie. Her smile became more free. "Give me a cigarette, will you?"

He lit one for her.

Bidot was driving as if he had been used to dispersing all the traffic in front of him for years; the car glided forward at increasing speed, and no one protested and no one seemed to get in the way.

"What really made you change sides?" Dawlish demanded.

"I've been on the wrong side for a long time, and you brought that home to me," she said. "If I had to choose between you and Maidment, I would always choose you. I couldn't see any future with Maidment, anyhow, so—oh, forget it." She drew at her cigarette, and settled down in the corner, while Dawlish tried to think only of the road ahead, not of the road behind.

Then Bidot said quietly, "I do not know if it is after us, but there is a police car behind."

21 POLICE MOVE

BLONDIE'S FINGERS TIGHTENED on Dawlish's. She did not look behind, but glanced up at him. In spite of the threat from the police, Dawlish was acutely aware of her tension. She had been screwed up to a high pitch of fear for a long time. She had played that sulky seductress as if it were part of her temperament, but all the time had been afraid. She had tried to wrench herself away from her fear, but for the moment all she had done was to exchange one cause of it for another.

Dawlish lowered his head.

Now he could see the car behind them, in the mirror. He knew that it was much closer even than when Bidot had spoken. He had never admired Bidot so much. His pale, gentle-looking hands were light on the wheel, and he neither hurried nor slackened pace, did nothing to suggest to the driver of the car behind that he was aware of him. When the road ahead cleared a little he pulled toward the right, to allow the police to pass.

Would they?

Blondie's grip was so tight that she was almost hurting. She stared straight ahead, and Dawlish saw the way her lips were parted, how her eyes were wide open, reflecting this new terror.

Had she committed some crime of which he knew nothing, to cause such fear of the police?

Dawlish forgot her. There she sat, rigid and taut, her fingers clamped to his, and yet he forgot her. For the police car was about to pass. He could not see the driver or any of the occupants. He knew the drill of overtaking only too well. This car kept close to the Rolls-Bentley, as the driver would if he intended to pull across its nose and stop it. There was no way of telling how Bidot would react if that happened. There he sat, hands gently guiding the wheel. A small car shot out from a road on their right, without warning, and he braked, not too sharply, and the car nipped across their bows.

The police car drew alongside.

A driver and five men were in it; one in plain clothes and four *agents*. Three seemed intent on the road ahead, two were staring into this car. They were staring at him, Dawlish, and at Blondie. Blondie began to tremble. She bit her lips, while Dawlish had to sit and wait and dread. . . .

The police car swept past.

Bidot slackened speed slightly, to let it draw well ahead. He did not appear to change his position, but for a split second glanced around at Dawlish.

"It looks as if we are having some of your famous luck, Dawlish."

"Luck," echoed Dawlish faintly.

Blondie had relaxed her grip, and leaned back; her eyes closed and her mouth grew slack. Her forehead and cheeks were shiny with sweat. Dawlish covered her hand with his, squeezed gently, then lit two cigarettes, and put one to her lips. She took it without speaking. He wished that he had a whiskey or brandy flask, but hadn't brought one. She would be all right, though. He himself was sweating from the tension of that chase.

Now there was comparatively little traffic.

"I think I know where that car was going," Bidot said quietly, and he seemed touched by the tension which had eased in the others.

"Where?"

"The airport."

"Yes, of course," Dawlish said, and felt almost sick because he hadn't thought of that himself. There would be this story of the big man, the English friend of a wounded Englishman, and the police would set out to make sure that he didn't leave the country. Stations and airports would be watched, even before the roads. He drew hard at the cigarette as they approached the airport, and soon they could see the low terminal buildings, and the outlines of several aircraft; one was warming up. Then they came upon the entrance where two uniformed *agents*, guns in their holsters, were standing.

"We shall drive past," Bidot declared.

He did not slacken speed, and the policemen gave them only a cursory glance. Now they were on the wide, open road, and for the first time Bidot put his foot down hard on the accelerator. The car leapt forward.

"We are on the right side of Paris," Bidot said. "We can be at Le Havre in two hours."

He settled down in his seat. Blondie looked up at Dawlish, smiling faintly. He nodded and squeezed her hand again, then settled back in his corner and closed his eyes. There were a dozen things passing through his mind, all the time. First, Felicity; always Felicity, and the fear of what might happen to her. He couldn't be sure how long it would take for that message to reach Trivett. He couldn't even be sure that when it arrived, Trivett would take immediate ac-

153

tion, for the Channel Islands were not within Scotland Yard's jurisdiction, and it would probably take longer to get things moving there than in an English county.

Why make imaginary troubles?

What would Maidment do?

He would arrive at his apartment to discover what had happened there, and he wouldn't go in. Maidment and at least two members of his crew were still free. There would probably be others.

How would he get in touch with the Isle of Silla?

Dawlish winced.

He didn't have to think, and was behaving as if he couldn't. There wasn't any doubt what Maidment would do; it was as obvious and inevitable as that the police would check the airports and the stations. Maidment now had one driving fear; that his part in all this would be disclosed to the police. And he had one weapon, and only one: Felicity.

He would head for the Isle of Silla as fast as he could and would take Felicity away. Once he succeeded, he had some kind of weapon with which to fight. He would be on his way already—and as the police were not looking for him, there was nothing to prevent him from taking an aircraft to Le Havre.

Blondie was looking at Dawlish's set profile.

"What's on your mind?" she asked.

He didn't answer.

"Why don't you tell me?" she urged. "Didn't you know that a trouble shared was a trouble halved?"

Bidot asked softly: "What is that?"

"Old adage," Dawlish said, easing his collar. "All right, I'll tell you what's on my mind. Are you listening, Bidot?"

"Attentively."

"Maidment will get to that island just as fast as he can, and if he can't take Felicity away, he'll try to make sure that I don't," Dawlish said. "Has he access to an aircraft, do you know?"

154

Bidot didn't answer for some time, but soon his fingers tightened on the steering wheel, and there was a slight movement of the muscles at his neck and the side of his face, as if this was a threat he hadn't thought of.

"Has he?" Dawlish asked roughly.

"He has no private aircraft, as I have," said Bidot. "But there are charter planes, and it is always possible to fly from Paris to Le Havre at short notice." He glanced upward, as if to search the sky; and not far away were two airplanes, flying away from Paris. There was nothing surprising in that, it was fantastic even to think that Maidment and his men were in either of them, but it was an indication of what could happen.

The speedometer of the Rolls-Bentley touched the hundred mark. The road ahead was quite straight, and the speedometer hardly quivered. They swept past traffic, through villages, over crossroads, and at the crossroads Bidot kept his hand on the horn. A few people stared at but no one tried to stop them. At some towns, he was forced to slow down. Dawlish lit the last cigarette in his packet, and flicked the screwed-up packet to the floor.

Now, they were driving straight into the sun, which was bright red in the evening sky. Bidot pulled the shade down, but dazzle added to the difficulties of the journey. Dawlish watched the signposts, and they seemed to swallow the kilometers until they came to a fork in the road, and a signpost said: "Le Havre—19 Kms."

"Twelve miles," Dawlish muttered, and said aloud: "Bidot, are you sure the yacht will be ready?"

"It is always kept in readiness, I tell you."

"So late in the day as this?"

"It will be ready," Bidot insisted.

Now, the traffic grew thicker, and the road went through straggling villages; they had to slow down. The town seemed to leap upon them, suddenly they were in the dock area, and Dawlish realized that there might be as much danger here as there had been at the airport. He didn't speak of it; Bidot wouldn't need telling, and there was no point in agitating Blondie any more.

"The yacht is tied up at a basin used by small craft," Bidot said. "We do not stay in the harbor for long." He didn't smile, although he knew exactly what that message meant to Dawlish.

They passed tall new buildings and huge sheds, and drove over bumpy bridges. Few people were about, but lights were on at a ship some distance away, and the signpost pointing toward it read: "Southampton Ferry." It was one night's voyage across the water to England!

How many hours to the Isle of Silla?

The Rolls-Bentley slowed down, at last. They passed some small, closed shops; ships' chandlers' stores. They saw a small basin, the water like a mirror, as it had been at Brighton, with dozens of small craft riding at anchor, most with their sails furled and their dinghies trailing. Several ships were coming toward the jetties, sails listless in the windless air.

Sails?

There were motorboats, too, and cabin cruisers, most of them tied up. On several, men and women were sitting or standing; here and there a sailor was busy, burnishing brass or furling sails or making ships secure. Near the end of the largest jetty, where only motor cruisers were moored, was a low-lying, sleek-looking craft, with two men aboard. One of these, looking toward the Rolls-Bentley, suddenly jumped ashore. As he did so, he made a gesture to the man on board, who disappeared.

"You see, it is ready," said Bidot. "We can be at sea in ten minutes, Dawlish. It is the first time that the *Claire* has raced an aircraft, but she is very, very fast."

Claire was painted in gilt letters upon the cruiser's bows.

156

22 THE CHANNEL

THEY WERE HEADING out to sea.

Bidot obviously had complete faith in the two members of the crew, whom he had introduced briefly as Georges and Charles. They were middle-aged men, obviously old salts, dressed smartly as befitted the *Claire,* and their faces were weather-worn with the wind and the salt-laden air and the sun of the seven seas. They went about their job with quiet confidence, and were not at all surprised when Bidot ordered them to put on speed. He had told them that they were heading for Silla.

The cruiser was roomy despite the fact that it seemed to be built like a greyhound. There was comfortable deck space, for lounging and sunbathing, and below were two two-berth cabins and a lounge. There a dozen people could gather, most of them even able to sit on foam rubber cushions. Every fitting was of first quality; everything that should shine, shone brightly.

"What will you have to drink?" Bidot asked Blondie, who looked around the cabin as if she was astonished at its luxury. She asked for a gin and Italian, and said:

"You haven't anything to eat on board, have you?"

Bidot smiled, and said: "Charles is preparing supper. It will be sufficient if not elaborate." He handed Blondie her drink. "Whiskey and soda, Dawlish?"

"Please."

Bidot poured out, and then helped himself to Dubonnet in a small glass, and moved toward a porthole.

"Shall we go on deck?"

"I think I feel safer down here," Blondie said.

"Why should you feel unsafe on board?"

"If I know Maidment, he might try to stop us," Blondie said. "He will probably guess what we'll do."

So she had a head on her shoulders.

"If he had attempted to stop us, I think we should have known by now," said Bidot. "He will take it for granted that he can reach the island first. And I expect he will." He sipped his drink, then offered cigarettes from a gold box. Blondie took one. But she didn't light it even when Dawlish held out his lighter; she twisted it in her fingers, and little pieces of tobacco fell out. Here was a clear case of nerves cracking in a moment of relaxation in the emergency.

Bidot took a light from Dawlish.

"Thank you." Except for being very precise, his English was that of an educated Englishman. "There is nothing we can do now until we reach the island, and I think it will take nearly an hour and a half. Le Havre is not the most convenient port for it in France. However, it will take Maidment some time to get in the air, even if he has chartered a plane. The airstrip on the island is north, and it will take at least twenty minutes for him to get from there to the house."

"*The* house?" Blondie exclaimed. "Is there only one?"

"One medium-sized house and several cottages, all on the southern tip of the island, which gets most of the sun," said Bidot. "The airstrip is on the north. There are no roads as we know roads, only tracks. Maidment might use a Vespa motorcycle, but the journey is over rocky land and any kind of vehicle has to be pushed much of the way. There is a good chance that he will not have much of a start, if any at all."

"Where can we land?" Dawlish asked.

"The jetty is near the house."

"So if we get there about the same time . . ."

"We shall reach the house first."

"That sounds all right," said Dawlish, and sipped his drink. "Still peckish, Blondie?"

"Peckish," she echoed, and then drew her head back;

there was a note of near hysteria in her voice. "Peckish! I'm starving. I simply haven't had anything to eat all day, just coffee and rolls at breakfast, and you ask if I'm peckish! What's the matter with you, why aren't you making the boat go faster? You're talking like a couple of cold fish, as if this was some tin-pot race which didn't matter a damn."

Bidot said, very quietly: "There is absolutely nothing more we can do, Miss Cunliffe." With a sense of mild shock, Dawlish realized that he had never heard that name before; and had not realized that Bidot knew her. "Georges is getting every knot he can out of the cruiser—I can assure you that the slight vibration means that we are traveling very fast indeed. We have to wait, and it won't help if we allow our anxiety to upset us."

Blondie said huskily: "Oh, I know. I'm sorry. I think I will go on deck." She tossed her drink down and then turned and stumbled toward the companionway. She walked up, slowly, her long, lovely legs disappearing, and they then heard her moving about over their heads. Dawlish pictured her as he had first seen her, when Felicity had told him that they were being followed.

"She will be all right," Bidot said. "I am glad that she has left Maidment."

"Has she known him long?"

"They have lived together for two years at least; she was on one of my longer cruises," said Bidot. "But I do not think that he ever intended to marry her, and doubtless she had realized that he would turn her away without hesitation if it suited him. She is not truly bad. I think I can understand how easily it is possible to come to dislike Claude Maidment," Bidot went on, and now feeling crept into his voice, and a look that might have been hatred was in his eyes. "I hope I shall meet him myself. If I do——"

"I don't think we'll worry about who gets who," Dawlish said. "First my wife . . ."

Bidot's expression changed, and he gave a wry smile.

"First your wife, and then mine," He brooded for a moment, and then went on in a very different tone. "My wife is quite safe from Maidment and any of his men, isn't she?"

"Quite safe."

"Where is she?"

"When we get back to England, I will take you to her," Dawlish said.

"I suppose that is as much information as I can expect." Bidot shrugged, then took Dawlish's empty glass and refilled it. He topped up his own glass, too. There was no sound upstairs, but noises were coming from below deck; it sounded like the clatter of plates and knives and forks. "I think that if anything should happen to Claire, I will kill her murderer with my own hands." He did not even glance at his hands, which had been so steady on the wheel of the Rolls-Bentley.

Dawlish remembered all he himself knew about Claire. Her beauty, her body, her simplicity, the fact that at times she was little more than a child; or acted like one. He remembered her as he had first seen her, leaning forward toward him on Felicity's dressing-table stool.

He could understand a man loving her for her beauty alone. Had she a mind, too? Or was beauty itself enough for Jules Bidot?

Bidot said: "We will have time to eat, and then we shall be very close to the island. We shall not be followed now. Do you think there is any chance that the police will have acted yet?"

"No."

"I think perhaps it is as well," said Bidot, and looked steadily into Dawlish's eyes. "I confess I cannot see how the future is going to work out for me, Dawlish. If Maidment is caught and arrested, he will tell everything, of course. His men are unimportant, he would tell them very little, but Maidment himself——" He broke off, shrugged, and then asked abruptly: "Where did you put the papers?"

160

He was deadly serious.

This wasn't a question put for effect, like that at his apartment, when the others had been within earshot. There Dawlish had believed that he was lying, but he couldn't believe that now.

Yet he knew he hadn't given Dawlish the papers.

Dawlish said: "Must we play on words here?"

"I am not playing on words. I am asking a simple question."

"I don't think I understand you," Dawlish said softly, and the tension which had eased so much when they had come aboard was back again; there seemed danger in the very air of the cabin. "I know nothing about the papers."

He was bewildered by Bidot's reaction.

The Frenchman actually lost color. For the first time, he seemed really badly shaken. His lips parted, there was momentary blankness in his eyes, which was replaced by a look not far removed from horror. It remained for several seconds, while the cruiser vibrated and the water splashed its sides. Blondie stood in the bows, hair whipped back by the wind that the movement created, while Georges stood at the helm, and Charles put the finishing touches to the meal that they were soon to have.

"So what are you trying to do?" Dawlish demanded.

Bidot said, almost hesitantly: "There is no longer any need to lie."

"I'm not lying."

Bidot said, with a catch in his breath: "You must be. Dawlish, don't——"

"I tell you I had never seen or heard of the papers until today."

"That cannot be true!"

"It is as true as I'm standing here."

There were spots of color on Bidot's lips and a glitter in his eyes; he had not looked like this before, and something in his expression set a warning bell ringing in Dawlish's mind.

"Dawlish, stop lying to me!"

"I tell you it's the truth."

"My God, I'll make you stop lying," Bidot rasped, and he snatched his automatic out of his pocket and thrust it forward, covering Dawlish's chest. He backed away swiftly, to make sure that Dawlish couldn't knock the gun out of his hand. His color had gone but for those two burning spots, and he looked deadly: as if madness had taken possession of him. "Now tell me where the papers are. Tell me where my wife is, too. *And stop lying to me!*"

Dawlish stood very still.

He said: "Bidot, I wish I knew what was worrying you. As I stand here, until you told me about it I had no idea what these papers were about. Until a man asked me for them last night, I never really believed they existed. That is God's truth."

The gun seemed to be quivering; it might be with the vibration of the ship. Dawlish noticed it out of the corner of his eye. He didn't look away from Bidot, because he was scared of what would happen if he did. The man was in a mood to shoot. In a few seconds he had turned from a rational, logical, self-possessed individual to a man who didn't seem sane.

His back was to the companionway.

Dawlish saw a movement there; saw Blondie starting down the stairs. She must have heard them, and was coming down stealthily, a step at a time.

"It can't be true," Bidot said.

"It's true."

"It can't be true! My wife gave you those papers, Dawlish, admit it. She gave them to you, and you have them. She brought them to you on my instructions, I told her that you were to be trusted. Now prove it. Don't lie to me any more, you won't get away with the papers even if you try to keep

162

them from me. I would see you dead first. Don't lie any more. Where are they?"

Dawlish only knew that this man's wife, who was so deeply loved, had not given him the papers, had not seen him until the meeting at Four Ways.

He also felt sure that Bidot had given them to her, believing her when she had told him that Dawlish had them.

"Where are the papers?" Bidot shouted at him. "Tell me or I'll shoot you where you stand!"

He stood just out of Dawlish's reach, and if Dawlish lunged forward, he would shoot. In spite of his rage, his hand was steady, and it pointed straight at Dawlish's chest.

The cabin seemed to have become very warm. The vibration was still noticeable, but Dawlish was oblivious of everything else—except one thing: Blondie. She had reached the foot of the companionway, and he could see her face, set tensely, lips parted. She was creeping forward, and there was no doubt what she meant to do; but if either she or Dawlish made a false move, Bidot would shoot.

"I'll tell you where to find your wife," Dawlish said. "If you wish, you can go and see her, before I do. You can ask her if she saw me or gave me the papers." He paused; and there was some relief, because Bidot was listening, and Blondie was drawing nearer. She was in the doorway, in a moment she would be able to stretch out and jolt Bidot's arm.

"Your wife is in a cellar, an old air raid shelter, at my home," Dawlish said. "A friend of mine is looking after her there. Ask her whether she told me and gave me the papers, Bidot. You'll believe her, won't you?"

Then a man cried out in French:

"Be careful, sir! Behind you!"

On that instant, Charles came in sight, leaping at Blondie, and on that instant, Bidot looked as if he would shoot Dawlish between the eyes.

23 THE ISLAND

THERE WAS ONLY ONE THING for Dawlish to do. He moved and struck at Bidot's gun arm. He had never felt that death was nearer. But Bidot had been startled by the cries from behind him, and didn't pull the trigger until Dawlish had knocked his arm aside. The bullet smacked into the wooden paneling. Blondie was struggling in the arms of the man who had come from the galley, and Dawlish's fingers closed around Bidot's, and twisted.

The gun fell.

"Bidot, I've never seen the papers," he said. "Stop behaving like a madman, and be a human being again. Charles!" His voice was sharp. "Let mademoiselle go."

Charles hesitated.

"I told you to let her go."

Slowly, Charles obeyed; but he didn't move away. His tanned face was set and worried, his eyes bright with uncertainty as he looked at his master. Bidot was standing quite still, like a man paralyzed with shock, and it was a long time before he broke the silence.

"It is all right, Charles," he said. "We are ready." He put his hands to his forehead and, for a moment, his face was hidden. Then he turned toward the companionway, and went out and up on deck.

"What was all that about?" Blondie asked bewilderedly.

"That's what happens to a man who believes that his wife has betrayed him," Dawlish said. "I don't know what she is getting at, but she certainly fooled him as well as me."

"Will he be all right now?"

"Except that he'll hate himself for losing his self-control, yes," Dawlish said. "He'll behave as if nothing has happened. The bad time will be when he meets his wife again."

"So it doesn't always run smooth," Blondie said in a choky voice. "Not even with men like you, and millionaires."

Bidot did not come below deck again.

Charles served a meal, a little grilled fish, beautifully fresh and of delicate flavor, and a steak which melted in the mouth, chipped potatoes and peas. Dawlish wasn't surprised that he was so hungry. Blondie was quite as ravenous as she had said; once she started eating, it was as if she couldn't stop. There were peaches and cream to follow, and the cream seemed fresh. The vibration continued all the time, and they were heading for the Isle of Silla and all that it might mean. Most of the meal, Dawlish had to exert himself to behave normally. He sat opposite Blondie at a small table which Charles had brought in; Charles served the meal as well and as courteously as if he was at the Carlton Grill or Maxim's.

Suddenly, Dawlish asked:

"Blondie, think back to Brighton. How did you guess my wife would take a dip?"

"Oh, we didn't," said Blondie. "We had to keep you apart for a while, that was all. Then you were heard advising her to swim, and Clem—one of Maidment's men at Brighton—was sent to get the motorboat, which we had for emergency use. If we hadn't done it that way, we would have found another. Maidment was so sure you had the papers, and meant to make you give them up at all costs."

Dawlish nodded.

Charles brought coffee.

"Let's take this on deck," Dawlish said abruptly. He didn't say so, but he felt stifled down here. Minutes dragged. Any time now, the island should be sighted; perhaps it was already.

Blondie went up first, Dawlish next, carrying coffee. They

165

reached the deck. Bidot was standing in the bows, immaculate, strikingly handsome and bleak. It was dark but for the moon, and the moon was very bright. The ship didn't roll at all, but cut through the water like a knife. As he drew nearer to Bidot, Dawlish saw a plate and a sandwich on a seat near him; so he had recovered enough to eat, if not to join them.

Somewhere far off were two brightly-lighted ships, but no other lights were in sight.

"How much farther?" Dawlish asked.

"We should arrive in about twenty minutes." Bidot spoke quietly, obviously in complete control of himself again. "We should see a light. You see, there it is." A light flashed, red. "There is no lighthouse, but a lighted buoy at each end of the island," he said. "It is not on any of the regular shipping lanes." He did not look around, as he went on: "Dawlish, will you please tell me when you first met my wife?"

Dawlish told him.

Blondie dropped into a seat and leaned against the gunwale, staring up at them; and the moonlight brushed her face.

"I see," said Bidot. "I am sorry I lost my temper just now. It is not pleasant to know that one's wife has lied. Please understand this: she came to England ahead of me. She was to see you, to give you the papers, to tell you that I would telephone to make an appointment the next day to discuss it. She said that she had given you the message, and asked you to keep the papers quite safe. I believed that she had. When I telephoned, you did not seem surprised to hear from me."

"I don't make a habit of sounding surprised," said Dawlish.

"She did not come?"

"The first I heard was when you telephoned me to meet you at Brighton," Dawlish said.

The red light flashed at regular intervals while the men

talked; the engine gave a muffled roar, and Blondie sat looking alternately out to sea, and at Dawlish and Bidot.

"You know what happened there," said Bidot. "I was told that I was wanted urgently in Paris—Maidment, who telephoned, persuaded me then that he was my friend. So, I went. While I was away, he persuaded Claire to go with him—or that is what he told me. It seems that he did not have to use much persuasion."

He stopped.

Dawlish, who had already heard the slight sound, understood why. The engines of the *Claire* still throbbed, but there was another sound, in the distance. Blondie was startled by the way the men acted, and stood up slowly. Then she exclaimed:

"That's an airplane!"

"That's right," Dawlish said, and he scanned the misty, starlit heavens, looking for the moving lights of an aircraft. Ahead, the red light flashed. Now people on the boat could see a yellow light, as if at the window of a house. That was all. The noise of the aircraft grew louder, and then they could see its lights, two green, one red. It passed some distance to starboard.

"So now it's touch and go," Dawlish said. He stared at the pale light on the island, then closed his eyes. He seemed to be praying.

Felicity was in the low-ceilinged room of the long, low house of the Isle of Silla. She was not secured to a chair but quite free to move about. The windows were shut and there were shutters on them, fastened on the outside, and the door of the room was locked. She had been here since she had first come around. It was in this room that she had made the recording which she knew would be played back to Dawlish. It was here where she had eaten and slept fitfully. Now and again during the day, the old man who was in charge let her out, to walk as far as the jetty and stare out to sea; no ships had come near while she had been there, and she believed that she had only been allowed out of the house when there was no danger of her attracting attention.

She felt numbed.

Even her fear was less than it had been; one could not live on the peak of horror for long. It had been some time since she had seen the snake released from the basket, and then put back into it. That had shaken her very badly. She knew that it had been done to put the terror into her voice while the recording was being made. Otherwise they had not ill-treated her.

The man who had brought the snake had gone off immediately afterward in a motorboat. She knew that there was at least another man, younger than her jailer, on the island; and, toward evening, a boat had arrived and two men had come ashore. She had not seen them at first, but she had heard them. They were somewhere in the house; occasionally she could hear them talking, but neither had shown the slightest interest in her.

She didn't know the time.

The only light came from candles, in wall brackets and old brass candlesticks. The old, battered furniture of the room was stained with candle grease. The walls were covered with plaster, but at places the stone walls showed through. There were damp patches, and unless a lot of money was spent on the house it would soon begin to fall to pieces. She had actually told herself that, and tried to imagine what it would be like living on the island.

Her chief fear, now, was for Pat.

She prayed that he would come, and yet was terrified of what would happen if he did.

Then she heard the men approaching the door, and stood up, heart palpitating. There was a pause outside, before the key turned in the lock, the iron handle moved, and the door opened slowly.

A tall man came in.

168

Perhaps it was the candlelight which made him look like a creature from another age. His face was like a hawk's; thin, bony, with a sharp nose and sharp chin. He turned to speak to a second man, who went along the passage outside, and Felicity saw this man's profile. The aquiline features had strength, and they looked as if their owner could be as cruel as an eagle with its prey.

He stood looking at her.

She stood at one end of the table, which was between them, her heart beating fast although she had tried not to show that she was suddenly at screaming point. She did not know how attractive she looked; she could think only of danger.

The stranger's smile surprised her.

"I haven't come to hurt you," he said. "I want to persuade you to help yourself." He didn't close the door, or attempt to come too near. He sat on the corner of the long table, smiling faintly, as if she amused him. "It is very, very simple," he went on. "Your husband was given some papers by M. Bidot, and I want them. That is all. Once I have them, there will be no danger for you or your husband. Why not be sensible, and tell me where they are?"

His English was so good that only an occasional word betrayed the fact that he was not a native. She was puzzled both by his manner and because he was so persistent about the papers.

"My husband may have them, but he didn't tell me anything about them," she said. "I can't tell you any more."

He eyed her up and down as if trying to decide whether it was worth making another effort. It was some time before he moved from the table. Oddly enough, until then his visit had eased her mind. Then, the other man came back, hurrying. Felicity saw him for the first time: it was the pilot of the motorboat which had brought her here.

"That was the doctor," he said. "Dawlish knows we're here."

Felicity almost cried out.

"He is coming. So is the doctor. If Dawlish arrives, he's to be killed. So is his wife." He spoke abruptly, and as if Felicity was not within earshot. "There is no safety with either of them alive. That is what the doctor says."

Felicity's hands, raised a moment before in a kind of ecstasy, were still held in front of her breast. She stared at the eagle-like profile, saw how the man's lips were set, knew that he was also frightened, of Pat.

"When will they be here?" he demanded.

"The doctor will fly. Dawlish is probably coming with Bidot, in a yacht. The doctor expects to get here first, but if Dawlish does, we know what to do."

"We know what to do," the eagle-faced man echoed, and he turned and looked at Felicity. Without speaking again, he went out with the man who had brought the message.

The door closed. The handle stopped turning.

The key turned in the lock.

The men walked away, and there was only silence, the chinks of daylight, the candles which burned so steadily because there was no breath of wind. One of them was very low; now and again the flame trembled, as if it knew that it had not long to live.

There was nothing Felicity could do but prepare to try to defend herself if they came here again; and almost certainly they would. She could pile furniture against her door, but they could come in at the windows, there was no way she could keep them out, she could only fight for her life.

And Pat's.

If she could only get away, if she could only get to the jetty to warn Pat when he came, she would feel that life still had meaning. But the door was locked securely, she had tried the windows a dozen times, there was no way to get out. Even the chimney was tiny; she had looked up it and seen a small patch of brightness at the top.

She had to sit and wait—wait for death.

She saw the daylight fading, at the chinks in the door and windows. It was still warm, but from time to time she shivered. Occasionally, she heard the men walking about the house, and whenever they drew near the door, she would stand up and grip a poker which she had taken out of the fireplace, but that was no more than a gesture.

If only she could be sure that Pat was safe.

The dying candle fluttered all the time now, and the light from it was very faint. The others burned steadily.

Then she heard a different sound, the unmistakable beat of an aircraft overhead, and her fear became acute. This would be the doctor; so he had arrived, while Pat was still at sea. Pat was coming to her rescue, and coming to his death.

24 THE RACE

THE SOUND OF THE AIRCRAFT was still very loud on the night air. Its lights still showed. The *Claire*, sailing without lights, was now much nearer the island, and it was just possible to pick out the shape of the island itself, black against the moonlit sea.

Dawlish was still standing with Bidot in the bows; Blondie was sitting down, and her eyes seemed closed.

"We may be just in time," Bidot said.

"Are you sure they'd keep my wife at the house?"

"Where else would they keep her? None of the cottages is occupied, most of them are falling down," said Bidot. "There is nowhere else."

Dawlish said: "How far is the jetty from the house?"

"Perhaps three hundred yards," Bidot told him.

They rounded a headland, and for the first time could just make out the shape of the jetty, and see several pale yellow lights ashore; all grouped together. There was the shadowy outline of cottages, too. Two or three small boats were riding at anchor, visible in the pale light.

Blondie stood up.

Dawlish said: "Bidot, I want you and the crew to take her to the jetty. Forget me."

Bidot said, as if astounded: "But your wife! She is——"

"In that house," Dawlish said. "You told me. But it's going to take a long time to get alongside, and the jetty may be watched. Getting ashore isn't going to be so easy. I want to make sure that one of us gets there." He was already slipping off his coat; and next he pulled his shirt over his head. "Don't run to swimming trunks, do you?"

Bidot said slowly: "Perhaps it is a good idea, yes. I will tell Georges to go a little closer inshore, and you would be wise to leave the ship to leeward. In five minutes, I should think. Go below, and ask Charles for what you need. There is a waterproof bag for your gun."

"Thanks," said Dawlish, and went below.

In four minutes he was back on deck, wearing a pair of swimming trunks, and with a small waterproof bag tied around his neck. The gun in it kept bumping against his chest. They were very close to the jetty, broadside on to the beach which showed up pale against the darkness of the sea and of the land beyond.

"Over now," Bidot said.

"I'll be seeing you," said Dawlish.

Blondie was staring at him intently, but she did not speak. He went to the side. Bidot steadied him as he climbed over. He lowered himself slowly, and was almost at arm's length before his feet dragged in the water. He flung himself backward, to get clear of the wake, and plunged deeply. A dozen powerful back strokes carried him away from the *Claire*, and he turned over, and struck out for the shore. He could feel fairly certain that the bay itself wasn't being watched; there could not be so many men on the island, and the greater danger would come from the jetty. There was nothing yet to suggest that anyone was aware that the *Claire* was so close. The engine sounded clearly, anyone at this end of the island would have heard it.

Was there any chance that everyone had gone to the other end, to meet the aircraft?

That would have landed by now. Maidment himself was on the island with the men he had brought from France. All of them would be armed. All of them would be in deadly peril from the police if he, Dawlish, or anyone on the *Claire*, or Felicity, were to remain alive. That was the stark truth. To save himself, Maidment must massacre everyone who had seen and could name him.

But the freak chance sometimes came off.

If Maidment believed he had reached the island a long way ahead of the *Claire*, he might be careless. It was possible that Dawlish could get to the house, find Felicity, carry her to the *Claire*, and that they would all get away before Maidment knew that he had been beaten.

Freak chances did . . .

He saw a flash of flame from a spot near the jetty, then another and another.

Men on the jetty were firing at the motor cruiser, and flashes from the boat showed that Bidot and the crew were firing back. Bidot might take it alongside whatever the cost; or might try to shoot it out and drive the men off the jetty before trying to get alongside. In the mood engendered by what he had discovered about his wife, he was likely to take wild risks. Against that, Bidot was a man whose life had been ruled by taking calculated chances.

Forget Bidot.

Think only of Felicity.

Dawlish was swimming with long, raking strokes toward the beach, which couldn't be far away but seemed to draw no nearer. He fancied he could hear the lapping of the waves against the sand, but that might have been an illusion because of the speed with which he was swimming. He had set out for the windows of the long, low-roofed house, but that seemed to have veered around toward his left. He knew the explanation: there was a strong current flowing, and in spite of his strength he was being forced away from the spot where he wanted to land. He had to fight the current. He made a conscious effort and turned head on to it, then put on a burst of speed which would take too much out of him if he had to keep it up.

Then one foot touched the sandy beach. He struggled to stand up, but dared not wait to get his breath back. He shook the water from his head and face, pressed his ears, and as they cleared, heard the sharp crack of shots at the jetty. The cruiser wasn't alongside yet, but its lights were on, one searchlight striking the jetty and the land beyond, showing small boats, upturned, behind which crouching men were shooting. The vessel was very close to the jetty; before long Bidot and the members of his crew would be able to jump ashore. But once they did, what would happen?

Dawlish stumbled up the beach. The sand was very wet, and at each step he sank deep. The wind, gentle though it was, blew cold against his wet body. He dried his hand as best he could and then opened the waterproof bag for the automatic; it had seven bullets in it, all he had.

He reached firmer, drier sand, where walking was easier. The cruiser still wasn't alongside the jetty. The house was much nearer, less than two hundred yards away, and Dawlish could see that the front door was open, could see a lamp close to it, on a table, and fancied that he could also see candles burning. He began to run, not too fast, because he needed his breath when he reached the house; there was no telling what he would have to do before he found Felicity.

Then another, much more powerful light appeared, beyond the house.

He knew on the instant what it was: the motorcycle which Bidot had talked about. Maidment or Maidment's men were on the way, and they would probably reach the house at the same time as Dawlish.

The bright beam of the headlamp showed up the uneven ground over which the motorcycle was traveling; and the still night air carried the staccato beat of the engine. Dawlish made his supreme effort to go faster, and as he did so saw another machine appear, its headlamp streaming skyward like a searchlight, then straightening out. Both headlamps snaked toward the house itself, and there was a risk that one of them would shine upon Dawlish as he reached the front door.

Stones cut into his feet, but he did not slacken speed.

The night seemed all noise; the beat of the motorcycle engines, of the cruiser, the rattle of shooting—the battle by the jetty wasn't over yet. But there was no sound or sign of movement inside the house itself. Dawlish drew closer, feeling grass beneath his feet. He saw the yellow light at the windows on the right side of the door, and at the door itself, and pale cracks of light on the left side. He could make out the shape of fastened shutters.

The motorcycles were much nearer, and changing direction. The tip of one of the beams touched the doorway as Dawlish leapt toward it. He did not know whether he had been spotted or not. He saw the wide passage which led right and left, with a doorway at each end and two doorways leading off. He swung toward the one on the left, and the room which had been shuttered, and he shouted Felicity's name.

"Pat!" she screamed. "I'm here! Pat!"

He saw the heavy wooden door and the key, in the lock on the outside. He looked over his shoulder as he touched the key, and turned. The motorcycle engines were shut off, but there were the lights outside, and one of them shone into the doorway. He did not doubt that he would be cut off, but here was Felicity, and he had that gun with seven bullets. Seven, remember.

He flung the door open.

There was Felicity, just in front of it, her eyes blazing with the wonder of seeing him again. In that split second, while death stalked them, all that mattered was that they were together.

He said: "Bless you, my sweet. We're going to have to run or swim for it." He turned away from her, toward the front door. "Keep close behind me. Watch the rear, they may come in the back way, too."

That was all.

They were together again, they might not live, but Dawlish was as matter-of-fact as a man could be.

No one was at the front door, but Dawlish felt sure that one or two men would be just outside. They would wait for him to appear, and would shoot him down, as they would Felicity. They would have a man at the back, too, guarding the doorway even if he were not coming to flush them.

Felicity was close behind.

Two shots sounded some distance off, and then there was silence.

"Keep very close to me," Dawlish said to Felicity, and reached the door. By himself, he would have cut and run for safety, but he did not know whether he dared, with Felicity. The silence outside seemed strange and menacing, as if nature had stilled herself, while these men fought it out.

Felicity whispered: "Pat, there's a shadow behind us."

He turned his head.

At the far end of the passage there was the shadow of a man's head and shoulders, thrown by a light which was out of sight. Then, Dawlish saw another shadow, of a weirdly long hand, an arm and gun. Someone was at the corner, and in a moment he would shoot. The only chance left was to run the gauntlet of the men waiting at the front.

"I'm going to run for it," he whispered. "I'll cover you

when I'm through. Get by the door, the chap behind can't do you any harm then, and run for the jetty. See the boat?"

Its searchlight still covering the jetty, the boat was now alongside.

"Yes. Pat——"

"It's the only chance we have," Dawlish said, and felt her body close to his. "I'll run for it, too. See that boulder, straight in front of the door?" No one could fail to see it, any more than they could fail to see the headlamps of the motorcycles, crossed now, to make sure that anyone who ran from the house would be caught in the spotlight for a deadly few seconds. "When I reach that, you start running. I'll shoot the lamps out."

On that very instant, one of the headlamps went out, there was a crash of glass, a shout from a man near it. The shot had come from the boulder, someone was there, help was at hand.

"We'll go together," Dawlish said. "Now!"

25 THE PAPERS AND THE TRUTH

DAWLISH KNEW THAT FELICITY would do exactly what he told her, would run at his heels so that he could shield her with his body. The fact that there was help made all the difference in the world. There was only one more headlamp left; if they could put that out, too, the chances would be even.

Dawlish ran out.

He saw the headlamp, turning toward the boulder. It showed most of the scene with great vividness. There was Maidment by the motorcycle with another man. Dawlish saw the eagle profile, and knew that the second man was the one who had questioned and tortured him at Four

Ways. He saw Bidot by the boulder; and Bidot showed himself just long enough to shoot at the headlamp.

He fired.

He missed.

Dawlish fired at it, and the bullet smacked into the glass, the light went out, and for a moment the gray night seemed almost black. No other shot came until they were close to the boulder itself. When they reached it, Dawlish saw Bidot again, standing up, staring at the men who had fired at him. It was a strange moment, vivid in the bright moonlight. All they had to do now was run for the jetty and for safety. Georges and Charles and Blondie would surely give them cover; not all of them would have been hurt. But Bidot seemed oblivious of all that. He was standing up, not even taking aim at the two men by the motorcycle.

"Run!" Dawlish bellowed at him. "Run!"

There was a sudden burst of shooting; none of it from Bidot, who looked as if he had been paralyzed. Dawlish swung around. Felicity was all right, and still running—and he didn't need to tell her what to do; she would go for the cruiser. He saw a man and a woman on the jetty, near the boat.

Bidot gasped, and began to fall.

Dawlish was now behind the boulder and out of immediate danger. He could hear Felicity running, and heard a man shouting. There were more shots, and bullets struck the boulder, chippings sprayed about. Bidot was on the ground, writhing.

"Maurice," he muttered, "Maurice!"

Maurice?

Then the searchlight of the cabin cruiser was swiveled around. It shone on Felicity but she was soon out of its range. It shone on Dawlish, Bidot and the big rock—and then on Maidment and the man with the eagle-sharp features. They were vivid in the bright light, and momentarily afraid; it was as if they were hypnotized.

178

Bidot stopped writhing.

He still held his gun, and Dawlish saw him take careful aim. His face was in the shadows, and he did not speak again; but he fired. The bullet struck the sharp-featured man, who pitched forward. Maidment still stood by his side, and then Bidot collapsed and the gun dropped from his fingers.

Dawlish fired at Maidment.

He believed that he hit the doctor, but could not be sure. He was sure that the other men were coming toward him from the side of the house. Another motorcycle appeared, and not far off a third one. Felicity was on the jetty now.

Dawlish went forward, picked Bidot up, and stood up. He placed Bidot carefully over his shoulder, feeling the warmth of fresh blood touching his own body, and began to run. Someone from the cabin cruiser gave him fire cover. He thought he felt a sharp pain at his foot, but couldn't be sure whether it was a stone or a bullet. He reached the jetty. There was Georges, waiting, holding the vessel fast; there was Felicity, climbing aboard. All Dawlish had to do was step aboard, and then drop beneath the protection of the gunwales.

With Bidot—dead or alive.

He climbed over.

Almost at once, the *Claire*'s engines went into reverse and the boat shuddered as they pulled away from the jetty. Three men came running, but as far as Dawlish could see, none was Maidment. Maidment was wounded, please God, and might be dead. Maidment—and Maurice.

Which Maurice? The one believed to have been murdered by drowning?

Charles helped him to carry Bidot down the narrow stairs and into one of the sleeping cabins. Gently, they put him on a lower bunk. Felicity hovered in the doorway, but obviously Charles could handle the emergency, and there was no room for all of them in here. As far as Dawlish could see, the bullet had caught Bidot on the left side of the chest, but he was breathing.

Then, Blondie came hurrying.

"Get out," she said, "I'll help him." She had water and towels, and seemed almost glad to have something to do. Dawlish saw that the back of her hand was bleeding; that was the extent of her injury, and she did not seem to be aware of it. He backed out of the cabin, felt Felicity's hand, and saw something he hadn't noticed before, hanging on the wall of the cabin. It was a photograph of a man whose profile was unmistakable. Eagle- or hawk-like, this was the man who had tortured him at Four Ways and the man who had been with Maidment on the island.

Blondie and Charles were bending over Bidot.

Dawlish put his arm around Felicity as they went up the stairs; there was hardly room for them together, and he pushed her ahead. He had to bend his head. The moonlit night greeted him, and when he was on deck he saw a most unexpected sight: three or four boats were heading this way, searchlights sweeping the seas.

"Look," Felicity said, as she leaned heavily against him. "That can't be more——" she broke off.

"That's Trivett, otherwise the long arm of the Yard," said Dawlish, with absolute confidence. "Coastguard cutters, probably. No need for us to worry any more, anyhow." He looked at Georges, who was standing quite steady at the helm, as if nothing had happened; he had cut down speed considerably. "Darling," Dawlish said, "our turn very soon." He hugged her, with a restrained strength which could not hurt, and spoke in French to Georges: "That photograph in the cabin down below, Georges, the man with the sharp features. Who is it?"

"That is a photograph of M. Maurice Dillon, sir," said Georges.

So Maurice, Bidot's right-hand man, had not died by drowning. Maurice had vanished, and had then worked with Dr. Maidment.

And with Claire Bidot?

Here was Felicity, close to him, and Dawlish could think of other things. He moved with her toward the stern. She said nothing, understanding the forces working within him. He sensed that all she wanted was the sanctuary of his strength and the relief from fear. They sat down, watching the approaching vessels, saying little. He was colder than he liked and had forgotten that he was wearing only the swim trunks.

Felicity shivered.

"You'll be all right," Dawlish said. "You needn't worry, my darling." He held her firmly, and they were still again. He thought of Bidot's rage, so near to madness, when he learned that his beloved Claire had told Dawlish nothing.

Then Blondie came on deck, saw them, and moved toward them. She stood for a moment, looking at Felicity as if she wanted to find out what quality Felicity had to mean so much to Dawlish.

Dawlish said: "Meet Blondie Cunliffe, Fel. She changed sides."

Blondie said, quietly: "I'm not sure whether I was wise or not. Jules is badly injured. If I know him, after what he heard of *his* wife, he won't mind whether he lives or dies. We must get to land as soon as we can, and get him to a hospital."

One of the other ships was nearly alongside.

"We will," promised Dawlish. "We will."

They landed at Bognor, and within two hours Bidot was on the operating table. Within three, Dawlish had talked to

Trivett on the telephone, and also to the local police. Police from Portsmouth and Brighton had set out in coastguard cutters for the island, and Dawlish now knew that Maidment was dead, that Maurice was injured to the point of death. Three men on the island had been captured alive, two of them when trying to get away in the aircraft.

Maidment could not tell what he knew of Bidot, now.

But when Bidot came around from the operation, to face life, he would have the bleakness of betrayal forever in front of him. Was Blondie right? Would he want to live?

Felicity knew all this and said quietly:

"If anyone can help him, his wife can. Let's go straight home, Pat. It isn't far, and you won't rest until you've talked to her."

"Yes, I will. But you and Blondie stay——"

"We're coming," Felicity said.

There was a glint of wry amusement in Blondie's eyes when Dawlish said resignedly:

"Yes, dear."

A police car took them home, traveling through the moonlit night at a good speed.

There were no lights on at Four Ways, but one came on as the car turned into the drive, and by the time they reached the front door, Tim Jeremy was standing in the doorway. He had his hand in his pocket, doubtless held a gun, and he could dodge aside at any moment; but he came hurrying forward when Dawlish hailed him.

"All right, Pat?" Tim sounded desperately eager.

"Fine."

"Thank God for that! I had a telephone call from Ted. He's only slightly injured, but he's as worried as hell. Apart from the minor fact that you're wanted for questioning about a murder in Paris——"

"Self-defense," Dawlish said promptly. "We needn't worry about that. Is Claire still here?"

"Of course she is."

182

"In the shelter?"

"Yes. I didn't risk giving her a chance to escape."

"You couldn't have been more right," said Dawlish. "How's she been?"

Tim looked almost droll.

"Well, you know what she's like. A kind of school girl Marilyn Monroe with dark hair. Sweet and chatty, and so grateful to you. Underneath it all, I'd say, worried as hell. She seems to be worried mostly about her husband."

"I think we ought to find out," said Dawlish, and went to the door beneath the stairs, opened it, and walked down. He entered the shelter.

Bidot's wife was lying on her back, fast asleep, looking angelic and at peace with the world. Dawlish stood staring down. He heard a soft movement behind him, and turned to see Felicity. She was tired, her eyes were heavy and red-rimmed, but she also looked at peace as she studied the sleeping woman, then looked at Dawlish and said:

"She's quite lovely, Pat."

"Lovely," echoed Dawlish. "Ask her husband." He put a hand on Claire's shoulder, and was not surprised that she started at once, and her eyelids began to flicker. He shook her more vigorously. She opened her eyes wide, and she had the shocked expression of a child woken from a heavy sleep; for a moment it seemed that she did not know where she was, and that she might fall off to sleep again, and never remember that she had been disturbed.

"Claire, I want to talk to you," Dawlish said. "Sit up."

She stared, uncomprehending at first, and then struggled up to a sitting position. The camp bed was too small for her. Tim had borrowed a pair of Felicity's pajamas, and Claire looked young and very appealing in them. She looked past Dawlish to Felicity, and then her eyes opened wide as she said:

"You have found your wife! But that is wonderful!" That came out as if with genuine delight. "I know she is your wife, her photograph is upstairs. I am very, very glad."

"That's fine," said Dawlish dryly.

"Is everything all right now?"

"No."

Claire Bidot went very still. The delight in her expression faded and she put a hand out toward Dawlish, as if to fend him off, with any bad news that he brought. It was a long time before she said in a whisper:

"Jules—Jules is not hurt."

"Badly hurt."

"No," Claire said, in a strangled voice. "No, please don't tell me that."

Felicity was squeezing Dawlish's arm, was obviously trying to make him ease off the pressure; but he did not want to make anything easy for Claire Bidot. He wanted to make it as hard as he could, for this must be a final testing.

"He is badly hurt," he said. "What happens to him now depends on you."

"I must see him!" Claire exclaimed, and thrust back the bedclothes. "Where is he? Take me to him, quickly."

"There's no hurry," Dawlish said. "He needs a message, that's all."

"I—I don't understand you." Claire's eyes seemed the largest and most bewildered-looking in the world.

"Claire," said Dawlish, "where are the papers which you told Jules you'd given to me? Who did you give them to?"

Felicity was still holding his arm tightly.

He did not know that Blondie had come downstairs, too, and stood with Tim, at the threshold of the air raid shelter.

"What does that matter, if he is hurt?" Claire demanded. "I must see him, quickly."

"Where are the papers, Claire? I know for certain that you told him you had given them to me."

"Yes, yes, yes!" she cried. "That is what I told Jules. He gave them to me, and said that it could mean the difference between life and death to him; he told me that I must give them to you. But I did not. Do you know why? I did not give them to you, because I was coming to see you when I met Maurice. Then I knew that he was alive. I knew that he was the one who was working against Jules. And I was being followed, everywhere I went. If I had come to you, these papers which were life and death to Jules would have been found, because Maurice would have come after me, and would have taken them from you. Also, I had a message from a strange man. He said that if I told Jules that Maurice was alive, Jules would be killed. How could I tell anyone?"

"Where are they, Claire?"

"Why are you asking? I have kept them safely because I believed that these men would not kill Jules while they wanted the papers. How do I know that you will not use them against Jules?" She glared at Dawlish, then suddenly waved her hands. "Oh, you ask, but you cannot get them. I sent them to Jules's bank, in London, addressed: "To be called for in person!" There I knew they would be safe. Could I be sure that they were with you, with anyone at all?"

Dawlish was already beginning to smile, and his eyes to glow.

Blondie was drawing closer to Jules Bidot's wife.

"Claire," Dawlish said, in a softer tone, "your Jules will get better. I think I can promise you that."

He began to chuckle.

"But why do you laugh?" Claire demanded.

"I was thinking that you have the answer to most problems," Dawlish told her. "Simplicity, from Simple Claire." He chuckled again, gripped his Felicity's arm, and turned to Tim, and said: "We'll telephone the hospital, Tim."

The operation on Bidot was over by then, and there was no reason why he should not live.

Dawlish opened the *Daily Globe*, some three weeks after the end of the affair, while Felicity poured out coffee for breakfast and looked contentedly out of the window, toward the lawns and the flower beds and the trim shrubs. It was a warm morning, with a slight mist and a promise of more heat. She looked at Dawlish, saw the way his interest was taken by something he read, and asked:

"Is it another world crisis, darling, or has Surrey lost?"

He smiled across at her.

"M. and Mme. Bidot started their world cruise yesterday," he said. "They're taking a certain Miss Lucy Cunliffe, as a kind of secretary-cum-lady's maid. Bless 'em all. Coffee, sweet?"

"It's in front of you."

"Oh, so it is," said Dawlish. "Sorry. I wonder where he'll leave his precious load this time."

"Leave what?" asked Felicity.

"Never mind," said Dawlish, and turned to look at the sporting pages.